BRICK FAIRY TALES

BRICK FAIRY TALES

CINDERELLA, RAPUNZEL, SNOW WHITE AND THE SEVEN DWARFS, HANSEL AND GRETEL, AND MORE

AS TOLD AND ILLUSTRATED BY JOHN McCANN, MONICA SWEENEY, AND BECKY THOMAS

Skyhorse Publishing

Copyright © 2014 by Hollan Publishing, Inc.

Skyhorse Publishing books may be purchased in bulk at special discounts for sales promotion, corporate gifts, fundraising, or educational purposes. Special editions can also be created to specifications. For details, contact the Special Sales Department, Skyhorse Publishing, 307 West 36th Street, 11th Floor, New York, NY 10018 or info@skyhorsepublishing.com.

www.skyhorsepublishing.com

10 9 8 7 6 5 4 3 2 1

Library of Congress Cataloging-in-Publication Data is available on file.

ISBN: 978-1-62873-732-5

Printed in China

Editor: Kelsie Besaw

Production manager: Abigail Gehring

ACKNOWLEDGMENTS

For our third *Brick* book, we would like to thank our wonderful editor, Kelsie Besaw, for her dedication to these projects and for being just as excited about these tales as we are. Thank you to Tony Lyons, Bill Wolfsthal, and Linda Biagi, for the continued opportunity to produce such a fun and educational series of books, and to everyone at Skyhorse for working so hard to put them out in the world. Special thanks to Allan Penn and Holly Schmidt for letting us have a billion Legos.

On a personal note, John would like to give a big thank-you to the Frog Queen. Becky would like to thank Professor Moebies, for reminding her why she loves stories. And Monica would like to give her warmest thank-yous to Mr. Hekler, for being the reason she writes in the first place.

On Fairy Tales:

Folklore and fairy tales have enchanted audiences since people first began telling stories. Before the cartoons with musical numbers and happy endings, even before the stories were collected into books, these stories were a part of a long oral tradition that passed down important cultural messages about right and wrong and good and evil. The tales in their original forms do not always end pleasantly, nor do they shy away from bloodshed and misfortune. Some are slapstick and clever, while others are nothing short of horrifying. Like any good story that is retold over and over, fairy tales entertain and enlighten us: they show us what scares us and what we value most.

The most famous collectors of these classic tales were Jacob and Wilhem Grimm, or as they are more widely known, the Brothers Grimm. As German scholars searching for cultural stories passed down throughout cities and villages all over nineteenth-century Germany, the two brothers curated one of the most extensive collections of folk stories ever known. They published the first edition of *Kinder- und Hausmärchen*, or *Children's and Household Tales*, in 1812.

The Grimm brothers first put the stories together to satisfy their scholarly interests in German culture and storytelling and did not intend them for children. After the printing of the first edition was met with little success and unenthusiastic readers, the brothers returned to the text and reworked the stories to appeal to a broader readership. Each new printing of the book contained new edits and carefully crafted additions to both enhance the stories and make them more and more acceptable for young readers. In the same way that stories told orally change a bit with every retelling, these written fairy tales have slowly taken shape into the beloved stories we know today.

On Brick Fairy Tales:

Classic children's stories now meet a classic children's pastime. We have chosen thirteen tales from the original Grimm's collection, some that you may know and some of which you may have never heard. The tales are played out with LEGO bricks, which are especially well suited to the sometimes absurd and often hilarious consequences of some of these stories' characters. Each tale is told in its original form and remains unabridged, and each of the photographs has been crafted with special dedication to the humor, gore, and peculiarities of the folklore itself. We hope you enjoy this modern retelling of the Brothers Grimm stories through many, many LEGO bricks.

Cinderella

The wife of a rich man fell sick, and as she felt that her end was drawing near, she called her only daughter to her bedside and said,

"Dear child, be good and pious, and then the good God will always protect thee, and I will look down on thee from heaven and be near thee."

Thereupon she closed her eyes and departed.

Every day the maiden went out to her mother's grave, and wept, and she remained pious and good.

When winter came the snow spread a white sheet over the grave,

and when the spring sun had drawn it off again, the man had taken another wife.

The woman had brought two daughters into the house with her, who were beautiful and fair of face, but vile and black of heart. Now began a bad time for the poor step-child.

"Is the stupid goose to sit in the parlour with us?" said they. "He who wants to eat bread must earn it; out with the kitchen-wench."

They took her pretty clothes away from her, put an old grey bedgown on her, and gave her wooden shoes.

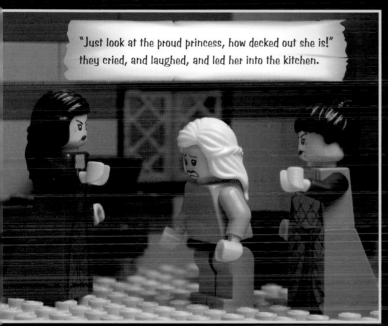

"Just look at the proud princess, how decked out she is!" they cried, and laughed, and led her into the kitchen.

There she had to do hard work from morning till night, get up before daybreak,

carry water,

light fires,

In the evening when she had worked till she was weary she had no bed to go to, but had to sleep by the fireside in the ashes. And as on that account she always looked dusty and dirty, they called her Cinderella.

It happened that the father was once going to the fair, and he asked his two step-daughters what he should bring back for them.

"Beautiful dresses," said one,

"Pearls and jewels," said the second.

"And thou, Cinderella," said he, "what wilt thou have?" "Father, break off for me the first branch which knocks against your hat on your way home."

So he bought beautiful dresses, pearls and jewels for his two step-daughters, and on his way home, as he was riding through a green thicket, a hazel twig brushed against him and knocked off his hat. Then he broke off the branch and took it with him.

When he reached home he gave his step-daughters the things which they had wished for, and to Cinderella he gave the branch from the hazel-bush. Cinderella thanked him,

went to her mother's grave and planted the branch on it,

and wept so much that the tears fell down on it and watered it.

And it grew, however,

and became a handsome tree.

Thrice a day Cinderella went and sat beneath it, and wept and prayed,

and a little white bird always came on the tree, and if Cinderella expressed a wish, the bird threw down to her what she had wished for.

It happened, however, that the King appointed a festival which was to last three days, and to which all the beautiful young girls in the country were invited, in order that his son might choose himself a bride.

When the two step-sisters heard that they too were to appear among the number, they were delighted, called Cinderella and said, "Comb our hair for us,

brush our shoes and fasten our buckles, for we are going to the festival at the King's palace."

Cinderella obeyed, but wept, because she too would have liked to go with them to the dance,

and begged her step-mother to allow her to do so.

"Thou go, Cinderella!" said she; "Thou art dusty and dirty and wouldst go to the festival? Thou hast no clothes and shoes, and yet wouldst dance!" As, however, Cinderella went on asking, the step-mother at last said,

"I have emptied a dish of lentils into the ashes for thee, if thou hast picked them out again in two hours, thou shalt go with us."

The maiden went through the back-door into the garden, and called, "You tame pigeons, you turtle-doves, and all you birds beneath the sky, come and help me to pick

"The good into the pot,
The bad into the crop."

Then two white pigeons came in by the kitchen-window, and afterwards the turtle-doves, and at last all the birds beneath the sky, came whirring and crowding in, and alighted amongst the ashes.

And the pigeons nodded with their heads and began pick, pick, pick, pick, and the rest began also pick, pick, pick, pick, and gathered all the good grains into the dish.

Hardly had one hour passed before they had finished, and all flew out again.

Then the girl took the dish to her step-mother, and was glad, and believed that now she would be allowed to go with them to the festival.

But the step-mother said, "No, Cinderella, thou hast no clothes and thou canst not dance; thou wouldst only be laughed at."

And as Cinderella wept at this, the step-mother said,

"If thou canst pick two dishes of lentils out of the ashes for me in one hour, thou shalt go with us." And she thought to herself, "That she most certainly cannot do."

When the step-mother had emptied the two dishes of lentils amongst the ashes, the maiden went through the back-door into the garden and cried, "You tame pigeons, you turtle-doves, and all you birds under heaven, come and help me to pick

The good into the pot,
The bad into the crop."

Then two white pigeons came in by the kitchen-window, and afterwards the turtle-doves, and at length all the birds beneath the sky, came whirring and crowding in, and alighted amongst the ashes.

And the doves nodded with their heads and began pick, pick, pick, pick, and the others began also pick, pick, pick, pick, and gathered all the good seeds into the dishes,

and before half an hour was over they had already finished, and all flew out again.

Then the maiden carried the dishes to the step-mother and was delighted, and believed that she might now go with them to the festival. But the step-mother said, "All this will not help thee; thou goest not with us, for thou hast no clothes and canst not dance; we should be ashamed of thee!"

On this she turned her back on Cinderella, and hurried away with her two proud daughters.

As no one was now at home, Cinderella went to her mother's grave beneath the hazel-tree, and cried,

"Shiver and quiver, little tree,
Silver and gold throw down over me."

Then the bird threw a gold and silver dress down to her, and slippers embroidered with silk and silver.

She put on the dress with all speed, and went to the festival.

Her step-sisters and the step-mother however did not know her, and thought she must be a foreign princess, for she looked so beautiful in the golden dress.

They never once thought of Cinderella, and believed that she was sitting at home in the dirt, picking lentils out of the ashes.

The prince went to meet her, took her by the hand and danced with her.

He would dance with no other maiden, and never left loose of her hand,

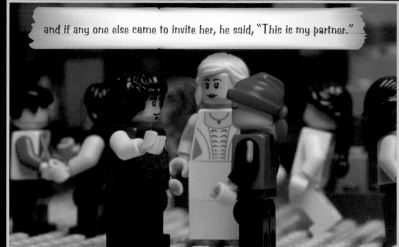

and if any one else came to invite her, he said, "This is my partner."

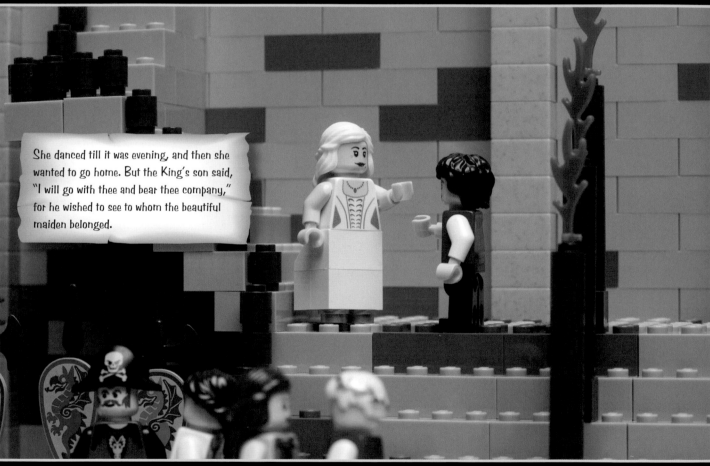

She danced till it was evening, and then she wanted to go home. But the King's son said, "I will go with thee and bear thee company," for he wished to see to whom the beautiful maiden belonged.

She escaped from him, however,

and sprang into the pigeon-house.

24

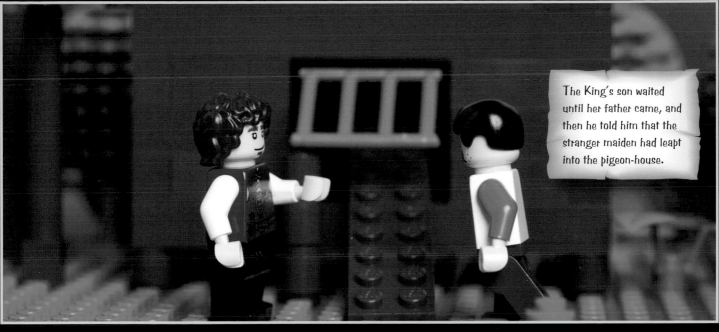

The King's son waited until her father came, and then he told him that the stranger maiden had leapt into the pigeon-house.

The old man thought, "Can it be Cinderella?"

and they had to bring him an axe and a pickaxe that he might hew the pigeon-house to pieces,

but no one was inside it.

And when they got home Cinderella lay in her dirty clothes among the ashes, and a dim little oil-lamp was burning on the mantle-piece,

for Cinderella had jumped quickly down from the back of the pigeon-house and had run to the little hazel-tree,

and there she had taken off her beautiful clothes and laid them on the grave,

and the bird had taken them away again, and then she had placed herself in the kitchen amongst the ashes in her grey gown.

Next day when the festival began afresh, and her parents and the step-sisters had gone once more, Cinderella went to the hazel-tree and said—

"Shiver and quiver, my little tree, Silver and gold throw down over me."

Then the bird threw down a much more beautiful dress than on the preceding day.

And when Cinderella appeared at the festival in this dress, every one was astonished at her beauty.

The King's son had waited until she came, and instantly took her by the hand and danced with no one but her.

When others came and invited her, he said, "She is my partner."

When evening came she wished to leave, and the King's son followed her and wanted to see into which house she went.

But she sprang away from him, and into the garden behind the house. Therein stood a beautiful tall tree on which hung the most magnificent pears.

She clambered so nimbly between the branches like a squirrel

that the King's son did not know where she was gone.

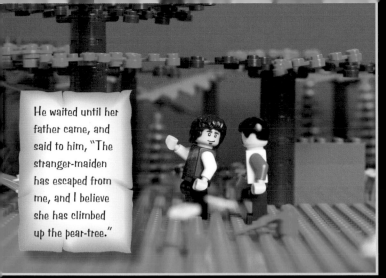

He waited until her father came, and said to him, "The stranger-maiden has escaped from me, and I believe she has climbed up the pear-tree."

The father thought, "Can it be Cinderella?"

and had an axe brought and cut the tree down, but no one was on it.

And when they got into the kitchen, Cinderella lay there amongst the ashes, as usual,

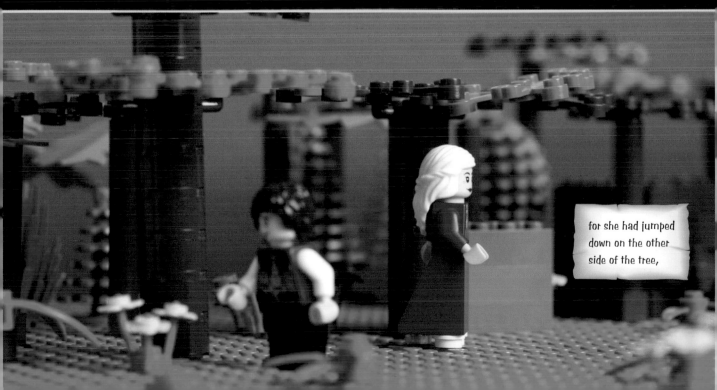

for she had jumped down on the other side of the tree,

had taken the beautiful dress to the bird on the little hazel-tree, and put on her grey gown.

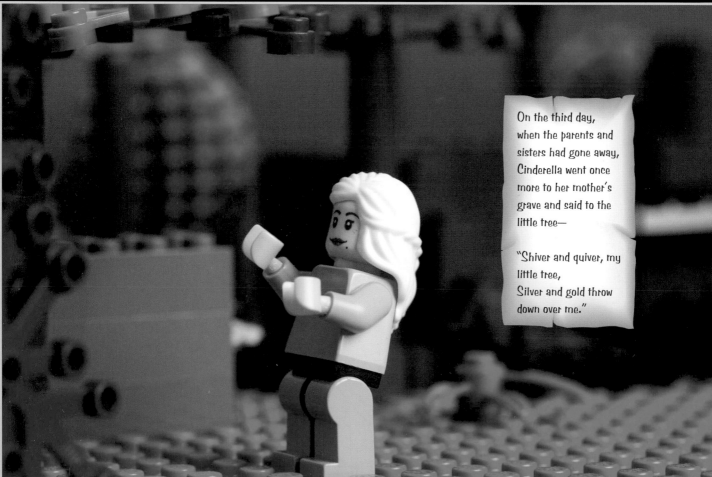

On the third day, when the parents and sisters had gone away, Cinderella went once more to her mother's grave and said to the little tree—

"Shiver and quiver, my little tree,
Silver and gold throw down over me."

And now the bird threw down to her a dress which was more splendid and magnificent than any she had yet had, and the slippers were golden.

And when she went to the festival in the dress, no one knew how to speak for astonishment. The King's son danced with her only,

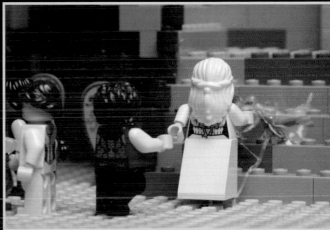

and if any one invited her to dance, he said, "She is my partner."

When evening came, Cinderella wished to leave, and the King's son was anxious to go with her,

but she escaped from him so quickly that he could not follow her. The King's son had, however, used a stratagem, and had caused the whole staircase to be smeared with pitch, and there, when she ran down, had the maiden's left slipper remained sticking. The King's son picked it up, and it was small and dainty, and all golden.

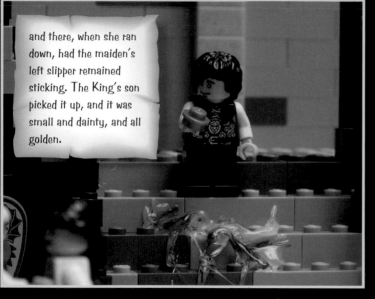

Next morning, he went with it to the father, and said to him, "No one shall be my wife but she whose foot this golden slipper fits." Then were the two sisters glad, for they had pretty feet.

The eldest went with the shoe into her room and wanted to try it on, and her mother stood by. But she could not get her big toe into it, and the shoe was too small for her.

Then her mother gave her a knife and said, "Cut the toe off; when thou art Queen thou wilt have no more need to go on foot."

The maiden cut the toe off, forced the foot into the shoe, swallowed the pain, and went out to the King's son.

Then he took her on his his horse as his bride and rode away with her.

They were, however, obliged to pass the grave, and there, on the hazel-tree, sat the two pigeons and cried,

"Turn and peep, turn and peep, There's blood within the shoe,

The shoe it is too small for her, The true bride waits for you."

Then he looked at her foot and saw how the blood was streaming from it.

He turned his horse round and took the false bride home again, and said she was not the true one, and that the other sister was to put the shoe on.

33

Then this one went into her chamber and got her toes safely into the shoe, but her heel was too large.

So her mother gave her a knife and said, "Cut a bit off thy heel; when thou art Queen thou wilt have no more need to go on foot."

The maiden cut a bit off her heel, forced her foot into the shoe, swallowed the pain, and went out to the King's son.

He took her on his horse as his bride, and rode away with her,

but when they passed by the hazel-tree, two little pigeons sat on it and cried,

"Turn and peep, turn and peep,
There's blood within the shoe,

The shoe it is too small for her,
The true bride waits for you."

He looked down at her foot and saw how the blood was running out of her shoe, and how it had stained her white stocking.

Then he turned his horse and took the false bride home again. "This also is not the right one," said he,

"have you no other daughter?"

"No," said the man, "There is still a little stunted kitchen-wench which my late wife left behind her, but she cannot possibly be the bride." The King's son said he was to send her up to him;

but the mother answered, "Oh, no, she is much too dirty, she cannot show herself!"

He absolutely insisted on it, and Cinderella had to be called.

She first washed her hands and face clean,

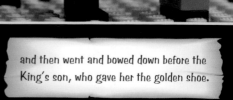

and then went and bowed down before the King's son, who gave her the golden shoe.

36

Then she seated herself on a stool, drew her foot out of the heavy wooden shoe,

and put it into the slipper, which fitted like a glove.

And when she rose up and the King's son looked at her face he recognized the beautiful maiden who had danced with him and cried, "That is the true bride!"

The step-mother and the two sisters were terrified and became pale with rage;

he, however, took Cinderella on his horse and rode away with her.

As they passed by the hazel-tree, the two white doves cried—

"Turn and peep, turn and peep,
No blood is in the shoe,
The shoe is not too small for her,
The true bride rides with you,"

and when they had cried that, the two came flying down and placed themselves on Cinderella's shoulders, one on the right, the other on the left, and remained sitting there.

When the wedding with the King's son had to be celebrated,

the two false sisters came and wanted to get into favour with Cinderella and share her good fortune.

When the betrothed couple went to church, the elder was at the right side and the younger at the left, and the pigeons pecked out one eye of each of them.

Afterwards as they came back, the elder was at the left, and the younger at the right,

Rapunzel

There were once a man and a woman who had long in vain wished for a child.

At length the woman hoped that God was about to grant her desire.

These people had a little window at the back of their house from which a splendid garden could be seen, which was full of the most beautiful flowers and herbs.

It was, however, surrounded by a high wall, and no one dared to go into it because it belonged to an enchantress, who had great power and was dreaded by all the world.

One day the woman was standing by this window and looking down into the garden, when she saw a bed which was planted with the most beautiful rampion (rapunzel), and it looked so fresh and green that she longed for it, and had the greatest desire to eat some.

This desire increased every day, and as she knew that she could not get any of it, she quite pined away, and looked pale and miserable.

Then her husband was alarmed, and asked, "What aileth thee, dear wife?"

"Ah," she replied, "if I can't get some of the rampion, which is in the garden behind our house, to eat, I shall die."

The man, who loved her, thought, "Sooner than let thy wife die, bring her some of the rampion thyself, let it cost thee what it will."

In the twilight of the evening, he clambered down over the wall into the garden of the enchantress,

hastily clutched a handful of rampion,

and took it to his wife.

She at once made herself a salad of it, and ate it with much relish. She, however, liked it so much—

so very much, that the next day she longed for it three times as much as before. If she was to have any rest, her husband must once more descend into the garden.

In the gloom of evening, therefore, he let himself down again;

but when he had clambered down the wall he was terribly afraid,

for he saw the enchantress standing before him.

"How canst thou dare," said she with angry look, "to descend into my garden and steal my rampion like a thief? Thou shalt suffer for it!"

"Ah," answered he, "let mercy take the place of justice, I only made up my mind to do it out of necessity. My wife saw your rampion from the window, and felt such a longing for it that she would have died if she had not got some to eat."

Then the enchantress allowed her anger to be softened, and said to him, "If the case be as thou sayest, I will allow thee to take away with thee as much rampion as thou wilt,

The man in his terror consented to everything,

only I make one condition, thou must give me the child which thy wife will bring into the world; it shall be well treated, and I will care for it like a mother."

and when the woman was brought to bed,

the enchantress appeared at once, gave the child the name of Rapunzel, and took it away with her.

Rapunzel grew into the most beautiful child beneath the sun.

When she was twelve years old, the enchantress shut her into a tower, which lay in a forest, and had neither stairs nor door, but quite at the top was a little window. When the enchantress wanted to go in, she placed herself beneath it and cried,

"Rapunzel, Rapunzel,
Let down thy hair to me."

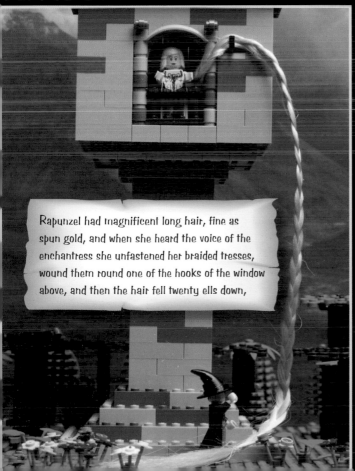

Rapunzel had magnificent long hair, fine as spun gold, and when she heard the voice of the enchantress she unfastened her braided tresses, wound them round one of the hooks of the window above, and then the hair fell twenty ells down,

and the enchantress climbed up by it.

This was Rapunzel, who in her solitude passed her time in letting her sweet voice resound.

After a year or two, it came to pass that the King's son rode through the forest and went by the tower. Then he heard a song, which was so charming that he stood still and listened.

The King's son wanted to climb up to her, and looked for the door of the tower, but none was to be found.

He rode home, but the singing had so deeply touched his heart, that every day he went out into the forest and listened to it.

Once when he was thus standing behind a tree, he saw that an enchantress came there, and he heard how she cried,

"Rapunzel, Rapunzel, Let down thy hair."

Then Rapunzel let down the braids of her hair,

and the enchantress climbed up to her.

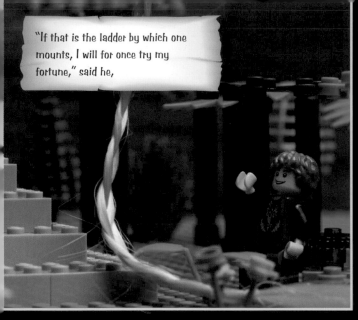

"If that is the ladder by which one mounts, I will for once try my fortune," said he,

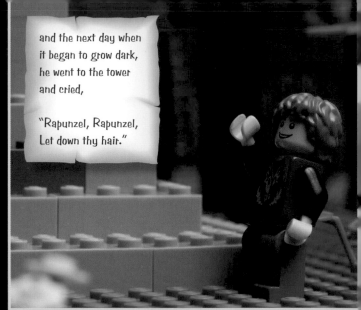

and the next day when it began to grow dark, he went to the tower and cried,

"Rapunzel, Rapunzel, Let down thy hair."

Immediately the hair fell down

and the King's son climbed up.

At first Rapunzel was terribly frightened when a man such as her eyes had never yet beheld, came to her;

but the King's son began to talk to her quite like a friend, and told her that his heart had been so stirred that it had let him have no rest, and he had been forced to see her.

Then Rapunzel lost her fear, and when he asked her if she would take him for her husband, and she saw that he was young and handsome, she thought, "He will love me more than old Dame Gothel does;" and she said yes, and laid her hand in his.

She said, "I will willingly go away with thee,

but I do not know how to get down.

Bring with thee a skein of silk every time that thou comest, and I will weave a ladder with it,

and when that is ready I will descend, and thou wilt take me on thy horse."

They agreed that until that time he should come to her every evening, for the old woman came by day. The enchantress remarked nothing of this, until once Rapunzel said to her, "Tell me, Dame Gothel, how it happens that you are so much heavier for me to draw up than the young King's son—he is with me in a moment."

"Ah! thou wicked child," cried the enchantress "What do I hear thee say! I thought I had separated thee from all the world, and yet thou hast deceived me."

In her anger she clutched Rapunzel's beautiful tresses, wrapped them twice round her left hand, seized a pair of scissors with the right, and snip, snap, they were cut off, and the lovely braids lay on the ground.

And she was so pitiless that she took poor Rapunzel into a desert where she had to live in great grief and misery.

On the same day, however, that she cast out Rapunzel, the enchantress in the evening fastened the braids of hair which she had cut off, to the hook of the window, and when the King's son came and cried,

"Rapunzel, Rapunzel,
Let down thy hair,"

she let the hair down.

The King's son ascended,

"Aha!" she cried mockingly, "Thou wouldst fetch thy dearest, but the beautiful bird sits no longer singing in the nest; the cat has got it, and will scratch out thy eyes as well. Rapunzel is lost to thee; thou wilt never see her more."

but he did not find his dearest Rapunzel above, but the enchantress, who gazed at him with wicked and venomous looks.

The King's son was beside himself with pain, and in his despair he leapt down from the tower.

He escaped with his life, but the thorns into which he fell, pierced his eyes.

Then he wandered quite blind about the forest, ate nothing but roots and berries, and did nothing but lament and weep over the loss of his dearest wife.

Thus he roamed about in misery for some years, and at length came to the desert where Rapunzel, with the twins to which she had given birth, a boy and a girl, lived in wretchedness.

He heard a voice, and it seemed so familiar to him that he went towards it,

and when he approached, Rapunzel knew him and fell on his neck and wept.

Two of her tears wetted his eyes and they grew clear again,

and he could see with them as before.

He led her to his kingdom where he was joyfully received, and they lived for a long time afterwards, happy and contented.

Little Snow-white (Snow White and the Seven Dwarfs)

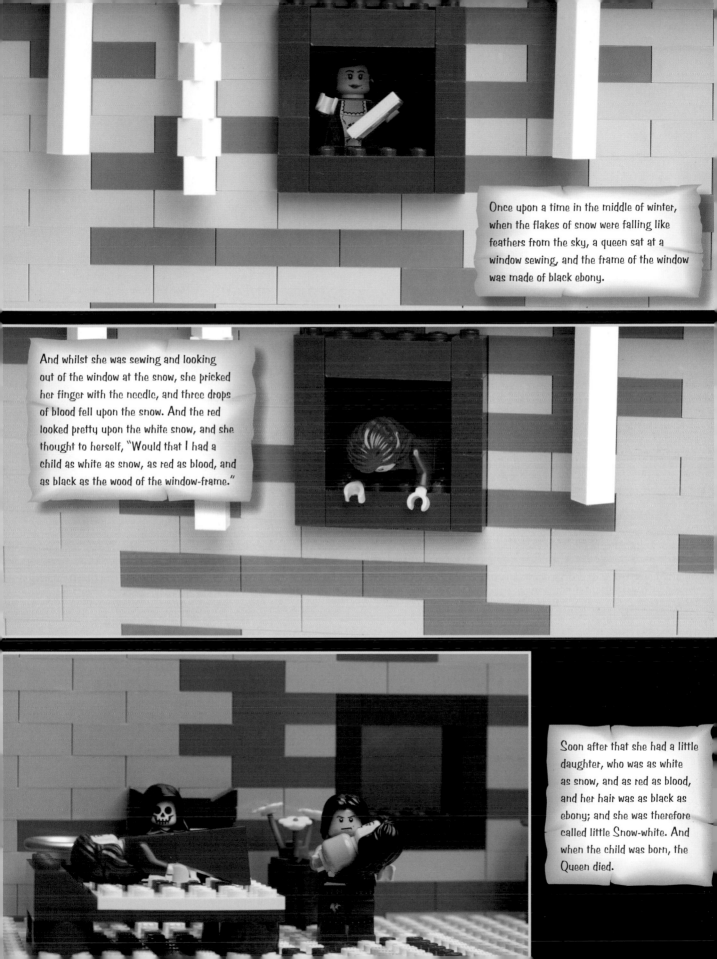

Once upon a time in the middle of winter, when the flakes of snow were falling like feathers from the sky, a queen sat at a window sewing, and the frame of the window was made of black ebony.

And whilst she was sewing and looking out of the window at the snow, she pricked her finger with the needle, and three drops of blood fell upon the snow. And the red looked pretty upon the white snow, and she thought to herself, "Would that I had a child as white as snow, as red as blood, and as black as the wood of the window-frame."

Soon after that she had a little daughter, who was as white as snow, and as red as blood, and her hair was as black as ebony; and she was therefore called little Snow-white. And when the child was born, the Queen died.

After a year had passed the King took to himself another wife. She was a beautiful woman, but proud and haughty, and she could not bear that anyone else should surpass her in beauty.

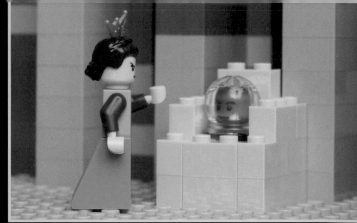

She had a wonderful looking-glass, and when she stood in front of it and looked at herself in it, and said—

"Looking-glass, Looking-glass, on the wall,
Who in this land is the fairest of all?"

the looking-glass answered—

"Thou, O Queen, art the fairest of all!"

Then she was satisfied, for she knew that the looking-glass spoke the truth.

But Snow-white was growing up, and grew more and more beautiful; and when she was seven years old she was as beautiful as the day, and more beautiful than the Queen herself.

And once when the Queen asked her looking-glass—

"Looking-glass, Looking-glass, on the wall,
Who in this land is the fairest of all?"

it answered—

"Thou art fairer than all who are here, Lady Queen."
But more beautiful still is Snow-white, as I ween."

Then the Queen was shocked, and turned yellow and green with envy. From that hour, whenever she looked at Snow-white, her heart heaved in her breast, she hated the girl so much.

63

And envy and pride grew higher and higher in her heart like a weed, so that she had no peace day or night. She called a huntsman, and said, "Take the child away into the forest; I will no longer have her in my sight. Kill her, and bring me back her heart as a token."

The huntsman obeyed, and took her away; but when he had drawn his knife, and was about to pierce Snow-white's innocent heart,

she began to weep, and said, "Ah dear huntsman, leave me my life! I will run away into the wild forest, and never come home again."

And as she was so beautiful the huntsman had pity on her and said, "Run away, then, you poor child."

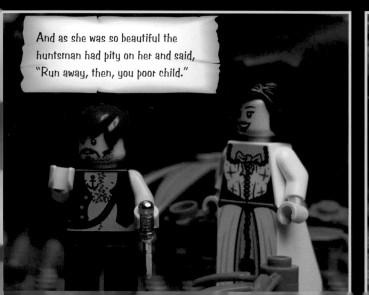

"The wild beasts will soon have devoured you," thought he,

and yet it seemed as if a stone had been rolled from his heart since it was no longer needful for him to kill her.

And as a young boar just then came running by he stabbed it, and cut out its heart

and took it to the Queen as proof that the child was dead.

The cook had to salt this,

and the wicked Queen ate it, and thought she had eaten the heart of Snow-white.

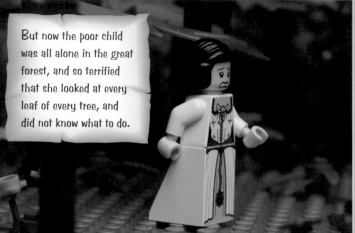

But now the poor child was all alone in the great forest, and so terrified that she looked at every leaf of every tree, and did not know what to do.

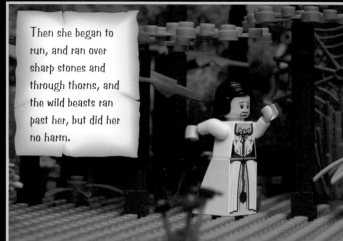

Then she began to run, and ran over sharp stones and through thorns, and the wild beasts ran past her, but did her no harm.

She ran as long as her feet would go until it was almost evening; then she saw a little cottage and went into it to rest herself.

Everything in the cottage was small, but neater and cleaner than can be told.

There was a table on which was a white cover, and seven little plates, and on each plate a little spoon; moreover, there were seven little knives and forks, and seven little mugs. Against the wall stood seven little beds side by side, and covered with snow-white counterpanes.

Little Snow-white was so hungry and thirsty that she ate some vegetables and bread from each plate and drank a drop of wine out of each mug, for she did not wish to take all from one only.

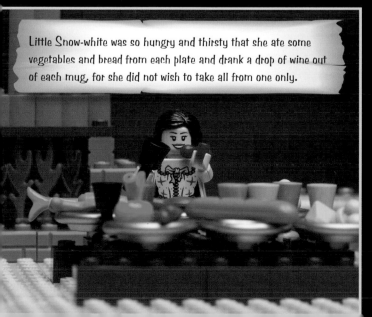

Then, as she was so tired, she laid herself down on one of the little beds, but none of them suited her;

one was too long, another too short, but at last she found that the seventh one was right,

and so she remained in it, said a prayer and went to sleep.

When it was quite dark the owners of the cottage came back; they were seven dwarfs who dug and delved in the mountains for ore.

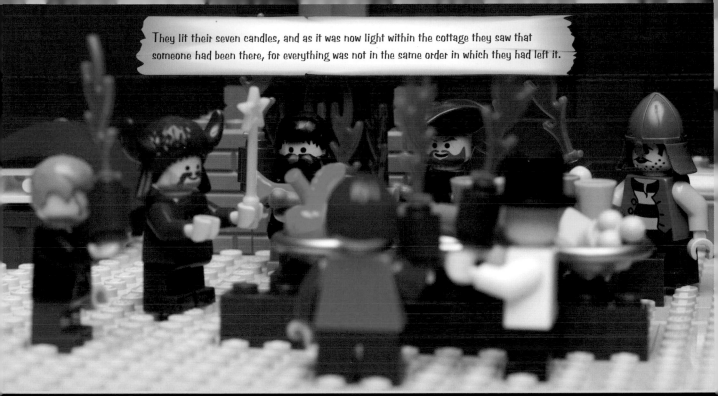

They lit their seven candles, and as it was now light within the cottage they saw that someone had been there, for everything was not in the same order in which they had left it.

The first said, "Who has been sitting on my chair?"
The second, "Who has been eating off my plate?"
The third, "Who has been taking some of my bread?"
The fourth, "Who has been eating my vegetables?"

The fifth, "Who has been using my fork?"
The sixth, "Who has been cutting with my knife?"
The seventh, "Who has been drinking out of my mug?"

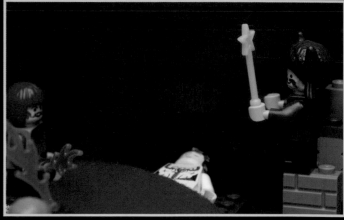

Then the first looked round and saw that there was a little hole on his bed, and he said, "Who has been getting into my bed?" The others came up and each called out, "Somebody has been lying in my bed too."

But the seventh when he looked at his bed saw little Snow-white, who was lying asleep therein.

And he called the others, who came running up, and they cried out with astonishment, and brought their seven little candles and let the light fall on little Snow-white. "Oh, heavens! oh, heavens!" cried they, "what a lovely child!"

and they were so glad that they did not wake her up, but let her sleep on in the bed. And the seventh dwarf slept with his companions, one hour with each, and so got through the night.

When it was morning little Snow-white awoke, and was frightened when she saw the seven dwarfs.

But they were friendly and asked her what her name was.

"My name is Snow-white," she answered.

"How have you come to our house?" said the dwarfs.

Then she told them that her step-mother had wished to have her killed, but that the huntsman had spared her life, and that she had run for the whole day, until at last she had found their dwelling.

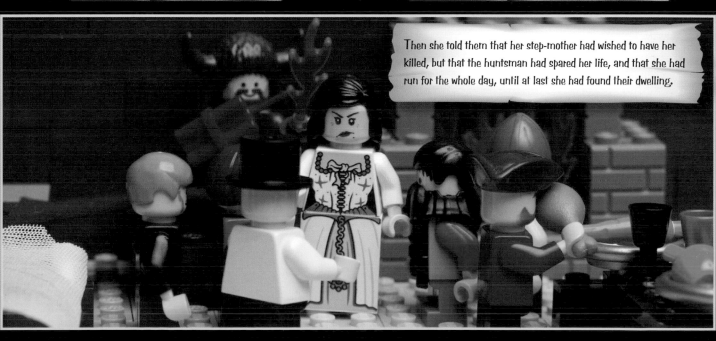

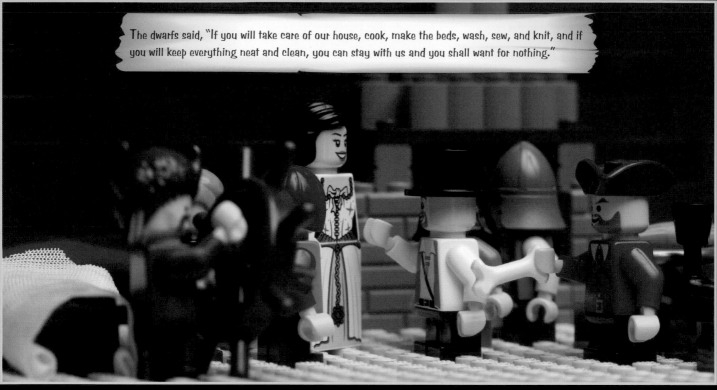

The dwarfs said, "If you will take care of our house, cook, make the beds, wash, sew, and knit, and if you will keep everything neat and clean, you can stay with us and you shall want for nothing."

"Yes," said Snow-white, "with all my heart," and she stayed with them.

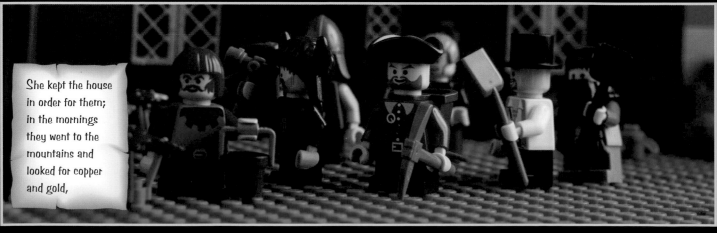

She kept the house in order for them; in the mornings they went to the mountains and looked for copper and gold,

in the evenings they came back, and then their supper had to be ready.

The girl was alone the whole day, so the good dwarfs warned her and said, "Beware of your step-mother, she will soon know that you are here; be sure to let no one come in."

But the Queen, believing that she had eaten Snow-white's heart, could not but think that she was again the first and most beautiful of all; and she went to her looking-glass and said—

"Looking-glass, Looking-glass, on the wall, Who in this land is the fairest of all?"

and the glass answered—

"Oh, Queen, thou art fairest of all I see, But over the hills, where the seven dwarfs dwell, Snow-white is still alive and well,

And none is so fair as she."

Then she was astounded, for she knew that the looking-glass never spoke falsely, and she knew that the huntsman had betrayed her, and that little Snow-white was still alive.

And so she thought and thought again how she might kill her, for so long as she was not the fairest in the whole land, envy let her have no rest. And when she had at last thought of something to do, she painted her face, and dressed herself like an old pedler-woman, and no one could have known her.

In this disguise she went over the seven mountains to the seven dwarfs, and knocked at the door and cried, "Pretty things to sell, very cheap, very cheap."

Little Snow-white looked out of the window and called out, "Good-day my good woman, what have you to sell?" "Good things, pretty things," she answered; "stay-laces of all colours," and she pulled out one which was woven of bright-coloured silk.

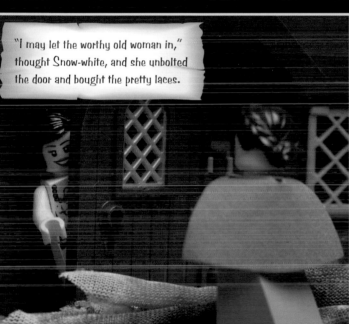

"I may let the worthy old woman in," thought Snow-white, and she unbolted the door and bought the pretty laces.

"Child," said the old woman, "what a fright you look; come, I will lace you properly for once." Snow-white had no suspicion, but stood before her, and let herself be laced with the new laces.

But the old woman laced so quickly and so tightly

that Snow-white lost her breath and fell down as if dead.

"Now I am the most beautiful," said the Queen to herself, and ran away.

Not long afterwards, in the evening, the seven dwarfs came home, but how shocked they were when they saw their dear little Snow-white lying on the ground, and that she neither stirred nor moved, and seemed to be dead.

They lifted her up, and, as they saw that she was laced too tightly, they cut the laces;

then she began to breathe a little, and after a while came to life again.

When the dwarfs heard what had happened they said, "The old pedler-woman was no one else than the wicked Queen; take care and let no one come in when we are not with you."

But the wicked woman when she had reached home went in front of the glass and asked—

"Looking-glass, Looking-glass, on the wall,
Who in this land is the fairest of all?"

When she heard that, all her blood rushed to her heart with fear, for she saw plainly that little Snow-white was again alive.

and it answered as before—

"Oh, Queen, thou art fairest of all I see,
But over the hills, where the seven dwarfs dwell,
Snow-white is still alive and well,

And none is so fair as she."

"But now," she said, "I will think of something that shall put an end to you,"

and by the help of witchcraft, which she understood, she made a poisonous comb.

Then she disguised herself and took the shape of another old woman.

So she went over the seven mountains to the seven dwarfs, knocked at the door, and cried, "Good things to sell, cheap, cheap!"

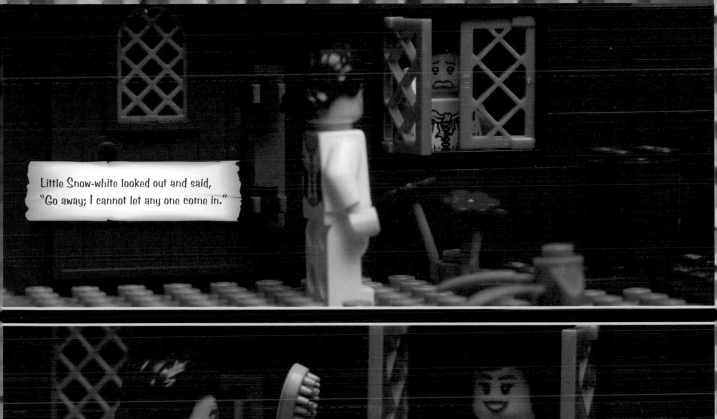

Little Snow-white looked out and said, "Go away; I cannot let any one come in."

"I suppose you can look," said the old woman, and pulled the poisonous comb out and held it up.

It pleased the girl so well that she let herself be beguiled, and opened the door.

When they had made a bargain the old woman said, "Now I will comb you properly for once." Poor little Snow-white had no suspicion, and let the old woman do as she pleased,

but hardly had she put the comb in her hair than the poison in it took effect, and the girl fell down senseless. "You paragon of beauty," said the wicked woman, "you are done for now," and she went away.

But fortunately it was almost evening, when the seven dwarfs came home. When they saw Snow-white lying as if dead upon the ground they at once suspected the step-mother,

and they looked and found the poisoned comb.

Scarcely had they taken it out when Snow-white came to herself, and told them what had happened.

Then they warned her once more to be upon her guard and to open the door to no one.

The Queen, at home, went in front of the glass and said—

"Looking-glass, Looking-glass, on the wall,
Who in this land is the fairest of all?"

then it answered as before—

"Oh, Queen, thou art fairest of all I see,
But over the hills, where the seven dwarfs dwell,
Snow-white is still alive and well,

And none is so fair as she."

When she heard the glass speak thus she trembled and shook with rage. "Snow-white shall die," she cried, "even if it costs me my life!"

Thereupon she went into a quite secret, lonely room, where no one ever came, and there she made a very poisonous apple. Outside it looked pretty, white with a red cheek, so that everyone who saw it longed for it; but whoever ate a piece of it must surely die.

When the apple was ready she painted her face, and dressed herself up as a country-woman,

and so she went over the seven mountains to the seven dwarfs.

She knocked at the door.

Snow-white put her head out of the window and said, "I cannot let any one in; the seven dwarfs have forbidden me."

"It is all the same to me," answered the woman, "I shall soon get rid of my apples. There, I will give you one."

"No," said Snow-white, "I dare not take anything."

But hardly had she a bit of it in her mouth than she fell down dead.

"Are you afraid of poison?" said the old woman; "look, I will cut the apple in two pieces; you eat the red cheek, and I will eat the white." The apple was so cunningly made that only the red cheek was poisoned. Snow-white longed for the fine apple, and when she saw that the woman ate part of it she could resist no longer, and stretched out her hand and took the poisonous half.

Then the Queen looked at her with a dreadful look, and laughed aloud and said, "White as snow, red as blood, black as ebony-wood! this time the dwarfs cannot wake you up again."

And when she asked of the Looking-glass at home—

"Looking-glass, Looking-glass, on the wall, Who in this land is the fairest of all?"

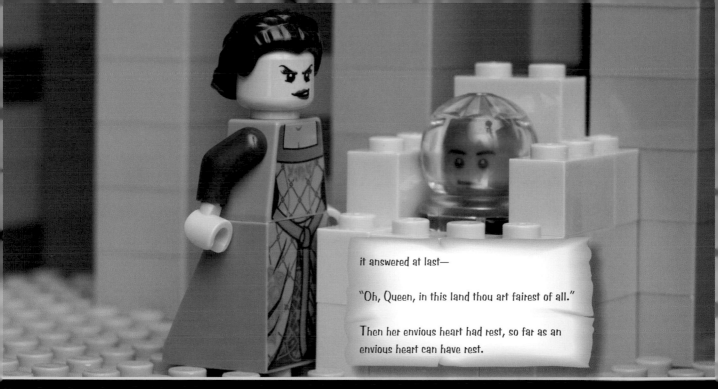

it answered at last—

"Oh, Queen, in this land thou art fairest of all."

Then her envious heart had rest, so far as an envious heart can have rest.

The dwarfs, when they came home in the evening, found Snow-white lying upon the ground; she breathed no longer and was dead.

They lifted her up, looked to see whether they could find anything poisonous, unlaced her, combed her hair, washed her with water and wine, but it was all of no use; the poor child was dead, and remained dead.

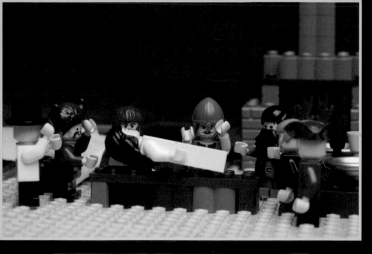

They laid her upon a bier, and all seven of them sat round it and wept for her, and wept three days long.

Then they were going to bury her, but she still looked as if she were living, and still had her pretty red cheeks.

They said, "We could not bury her in the dark ground," and they had a transparent coffin of glass made, so that she could be seen from all sides, and they laid her in it,

and wrote her name upon it in golden letters, and that she was a king's daughter. Then they put the coffin out upon the mountain, and one of them always stayed by it and watched it.

And birds came too, and wept for Snow-white; first an owl, then a raven, and last a dove.

And now Snow-white lay a long, long time in the coffin, and she did not change, but looked as if she were asleep; for she was as white as snow, as red as blood, and her hair was as black as ebony.

It happened, however, that a king's son came into the forest, and went to the dwarfs' house to spend the night. He saw the coffin on the mountain, and the beautiful Snow-white within it, and read what was written upon it in golden letters.

Then he said to the dwarfs, "Let me have the coffin, I will give you whatever you want for it."

But the dwarfs answered, "We will not part with it for all the gold in the world."

Then he said, "Let me have it as a gift, for I cannot live without seeing Snow-white. I will honour and prize her as my dearest possession."

As he spoke in this way the good dwarfs took pity upon him, and gave him the coffin.

And now the King's son had it carried away by his servants on their shoulders.

And it happened that they stumbled over a tree-stump,

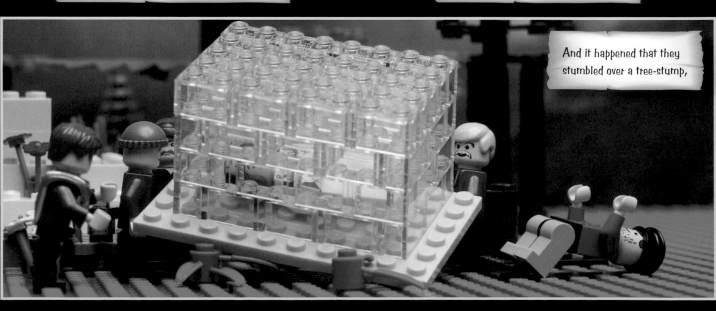

and with the shock the poisonous piece of apple which Snow-white had bitten off came out of her throat.

And before long she opened her eyes, lifted up the lid of the coffin, sat up, and was once more alive. "Oh, heavens, where am I?" she cried.

The King's son, full of joy, said, "You are with me," and told her what had happened, and said, "I love you more than everything in the world; come with me to my father's palace, you shall be my wife." And Snow-white was willing, and went with him, and their wedding was held with great show and splendour.

But Snow-white's wicked step-mother was also bidden to the feast. When she had arrayed herself in beautiful clothes she went before the Looking-glass, and said—

"Looking-glass, Looking-glass, on the wall,
Who in this land is the fairest of all?"

the glass answered—

"Oh, Queen, of all here the fairest art thou,
But the young Queen is fairer by far as I trow."

At first she would not go to the wedding at all, but she had no peace, and must go to see the young Queen. And when she went in she knew Snow-white; and she stood still with rage and fear, and could not stir.

But iron slippers had already been put upon the fire, and they were brought in with tongs, and set before her. Then she was forced to put on the red-hot shoes,

and dance

until she dropped down dead.

Hansel and Gretel

Hard by a great forest dwelt a poor wood-cutter with his wife and his two children. The boy was called Hansel and the girl Gretel. He had little to bite and to break, and once when great scarcity fell on the land, he could no longer procure daily bread.

Now when he thought over this by night in his bed, and tossed about in his anxiety, he groaned and said to his wife, "What is to become of us? How are we to feed our poor children, when we no longer have anything even for ourselves?"

"I'll tell you what, husband," answered the woman, "Early to-morrow morning we will take the children out into the forest to where it is the thickest, there we will light a fire for them, and give each of them one piece of bread more, and then we will go to our work and leave them alone. They will not find the way home again, and we shall be rid of them."

"No, wife," said the man, "I will not do that; how can I bear to leave my children alone in the forest?—

the wild animals would soon come and tear them to pieces."

"But I feel very sorry for the poor children, all the same," said the man.

"O, thou fool!" said she, "Then we must all four die of hunger, thou mayest as well plane the planks for our coffins," and she left him no peace until he consented.

The two children had also not been able to sleep for hunger, and had heard what their step-mother had said to their father.

Gretel wept bitter tears, and said to Hansel, "Now all is over with us."

"Be quiet, Gretel," said Hansel, "do not distress thyself, I will soon find a way to help us."

And when the old folks had fallen asleep, he got up, put on his little coat, opened the door below, and crept outside. The moon shone brightly, and the white pebbles which lay in front of the house glittered like real silver pennies.

Hansel stooped and put as many of them in the little pocket of his coat as he could possibly get in.

Then he went back and said to Gretel, "Be comforted, dear little sister, and sleep in peace, God will not forsake us,"

and he lay down again in his bed.

When day dawned, but before the sun had risen, the woman came and awoke the two children, saying "Get up, you sluggards! we are going into the forest to fetch wood."

She gave each a little piece of bread, and said, "There is something for your dinner, but do not eat it up before then, for you will get nothing else." Gretel took the bread under her apron, as Hansel had the stones in his pocket.

Then they all set out together on the way to the forest.

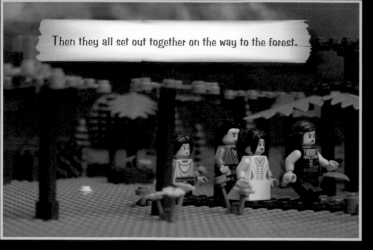

When they had walked a short time, Hansel stood still and peeped back at the house, and did so again and again.

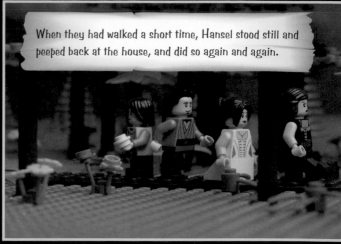

His father said, "Hansel, what art thou looking at there and staying behind for? Mind what thou art about, and do not forget how to use thy legs."

"Ah, father," said Hansel, "I am looking at my little white cat, which is sitting up on the roof, and wants to say good-bye to me."

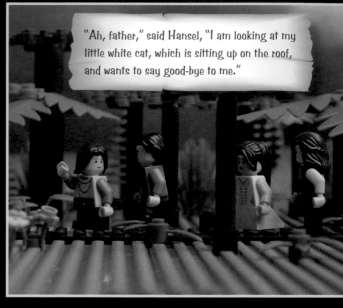

The wife said, "Fool, that is not thy little cat, that is the morning sun which is shining on the chimneys." Hansel, however, had not been looking back at the cat, but had been constantly throwing one of the white pebble-stones out of his pocket on the road.

When they had reached the middle of the forest, the father said, "Now, children, pile up some wood, and I will light a fire that you may not be cold." Hansel and Gretel gathered brushwood together, as high as a little hill.

The brushwood was lighted, and when the flames were burning very high, the woman said, "Now, children, lay yourselves down by the fire and rest, we will go into the forest and cut some wood. When we have done, we will come back and fetch you away."

Hansel and Gretel sat by the fire, and when noon came, each ate a little piece of bread, and as they heard the strokes of the wood-axe they believed that their father was near.

It was not, however, the axe, it was a branch which he had fastened to a withered tree which the wind was blowing backwards and forwards.

And as they had been sitting such a long time, their eyes shut with fatigue, and they fell fast asleep.

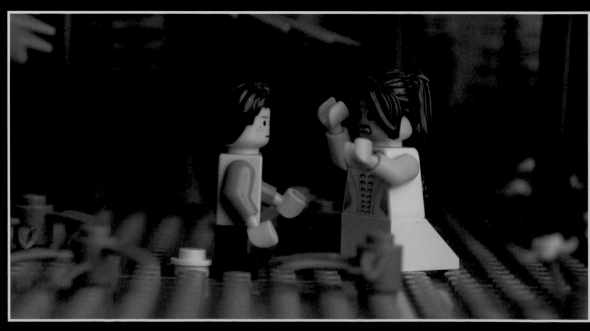

When at last they awoke, it was already dark night. Gretel began to cry and said, "How are we to get out of the forest now?"

But Hansel comforted her and said, "Just wait a little, until the moon has risen, and then we will soon find the way."

And when the full moon had risen, Hansel took his little sister by the hand, and followed the pebbles which shone like newly-coined silver pieces, and showed them the way.

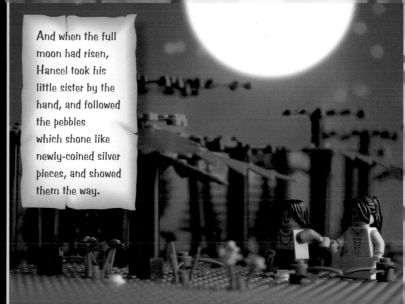

They walked the whole night long, and by break of day came once more to their father's house.

They knocked at the door, and when the woman opened it and saw that it was Hansel and Gretel, she said, "You naughty children, why have you slept so long in the forest?—we thought you were never coming back at all!"

The father, however, rejoiced, for it had cut him to the heart to leave them behind alone.

Not long afterwards, there was once more great scarcity in all parts, and the children heard their mother saying at night to their father, "Everything is eaten again, we have one half loaf left, and after that there is an end. The children must go, we will take them farther into the wood, so that they will not find their way out again; there is no other means of saving ourselves!"

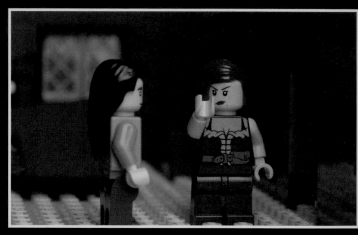

The man's heart was heavy, and he thought "it would be better for thee to share the last mouthful with thy children."

The woman, however, would listen to nothing that he had to say, but scolded and reproached him. He who says A must say B, likewise, and as he had yielded the first time, he had to do so a second time also.

The children were, however, still awake and had heard the conversation. When the old folks were asleep, Hansel again got up, and wanted to go out and pick up pebbles as he had done before, but the woman had locked the door, and Hansel could not get out.

Nevertheless he comforted his little sister, and said, "Do not cry, Gretel, go to sleep quietly, the good God will help us."

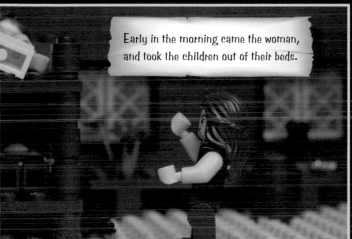

Early in the morning came the woman, and took the children out of their beds.

Their bit of bread was given to them, but it was still smaller than the time before.

On the way into the forest Hansel crumbled his in his pocket, and often stood still and threw a morsel on the ground.

"Hansel, why dost thou stop and look round?" said the father, "go on."

"I am looking back at my little pigeon which is sitting on the roof, and wants to say good-bye to me," answered Hansel.

"Simpleton!" said the woman, "that is not thy little pigeon, that is the morning sun that is shining on the chimney." Hansel, however, little by little, threw all the crumbs on the path.

The woman led the children still deeper into the forest, where they had never in their lives been before.

Then a great fire was again made, and the mother said, "Just sit there, you children, and when you are tired you may sleep a little; we are going into the forest to cut wood, and in the evening when we are done, we will come and fetch you away."

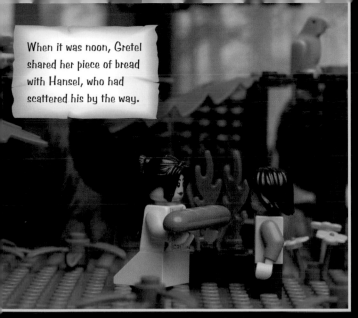

When it was noon, Gretel shared her piece of bread with Hansel, who had scattered his by the way.

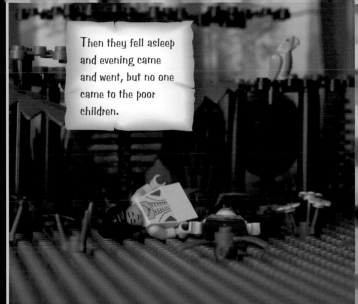

Then they fell asleep and evening came and went, but no one came to the poor children.

They did not awake until it was dark night, and Hansel comforted his little sister and said, "Just wait, Gretel, until the moon rises, and then we shall see the crumbs of bread which I have strewn about, they will show us our way home again."

When the moon came they set out, but they found no crumbs,

for the many thousands of birds which fly about in the woods and fields had picked them all up.

Hansel said to Gretel, "We shall soon find the way," but they did not find it.

They walked the whole night and all the next day too from morning till evening, but they did not get out of the forest, and were very hungry, for they had nothing to eat but two or three berries, which grew on the ground.

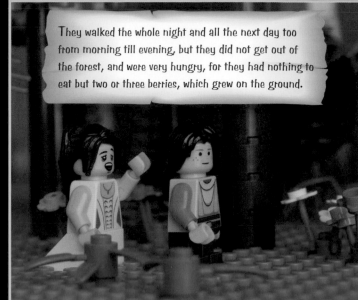

And as they were so weary that their legs would carry them no longer, they lay down beneath a tree and fell asleep.

It was now three mornings since they had left their father's house. They began to walk again, but they always got deeper into the forest, and if help did not come soon, they must die of hunger and weariness. When it was mid-day, they saw a beautiful snow-white bird sitting on a bough, which sang so delightfully that they stood still and listened to it.

And when it had finished its song, it spread its wings and flew away before them,

and they followed it until they reached a little house, on the roof of which it alighted; and when they came quite up to the little house they saw that it was built of bread and covered with cakes, but that the windows were of clear sugar.

"We will set to work on that," said Hansel, "and have a good meal. I will eat a bit of the roof, and thou, Gretel, canst eat some of the window, it will taste sweet."

Hansel reached up above, and broke off a little of the roof to try how it tasted, and Gretel leant against the window and nibbled at the panes.

Then a soft voice cried from the room,

"Nibble, nibble, gnaw,
Who is nibbling at my little house?"

The children answered,

"The wind, the wind,
The heaven-born wind,"

and went on eating without disturbing themselves. Hansel, who thought the roof tasted very nice, tore down a great piece of it, and Gretel pushed out the whole of one round window-pane, sat down, and enjoyed herself with it.

Suddenly the door opened, and a very, very old woman, who supported herself on crutches, came creeping out. Hansel and Gretel were so terribly frightened that they let fall what they had in their hands.

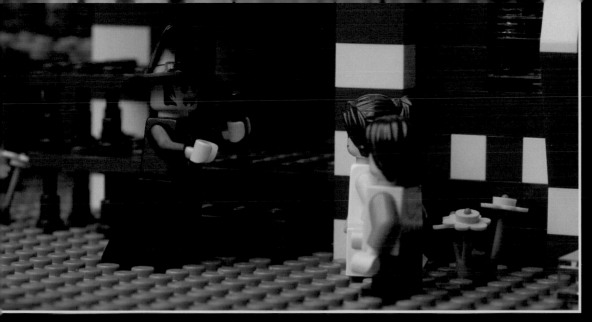

The old woman, however, nodded her head, and said, "Oh, you dear children, who has brought you here? Do come in, and stay with me. No harm shall happen to you." She took them both by the hand, and led them into her little house.

Then good food was set before them, milk and pancakes, with sugar, apples, and nuts.

Afterwards two pretty little beds were covered with clean white linen, and Hansel and Gretel lay down in them, and thought they were in heaven.

The old woman had only pretended to be so kind; she was in reality a wicked witch, who lay in wait for children, and had only built the little house of bread in order to entice them there. When a child fell into her power, she killed it, cooked and ate it, and that was a feast day with her.

Witches have red eyes, and cannot see far, but they have a keen scent like the beasts, and are aware when human beings draw near. When Hansel and Gretel came into her neighborhood, she laughed maliciously, and said mockingly, "I have them, they shall not escape me again!"

Early in the morning before the children were awake, she was already up, and when she saw both of them sleeping and looking so pretty, with their plump red cheeks, she muttered to herself, "That will be a dainty mouthful!"

Then she seized Hansel with her shrivelled hand,

carried him into a little stable, and shut him in with a grated door.

He might scream as he liked, that was of no use.

Then she went to Gretel, shook her till she awoke, and cried, "Get up, lazy thing, fetch some water, and cook something good for thy brother, he is in the stable outside, and is to be made fat. When he is fat, I will eat him."

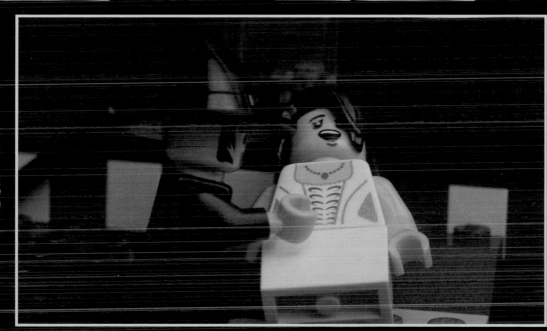

Gretel began to weep bitterly, but it was all in vain, she was forced to do what the wicked witch ordered her.

And now the best food was cooked for poor Hansel, but Gretel got nothing but crab-shells.

Every morning the woman crept to the little stable, and cried, "Hansel, stretch out thy finger that I may feel if thou wilt soon be fat."

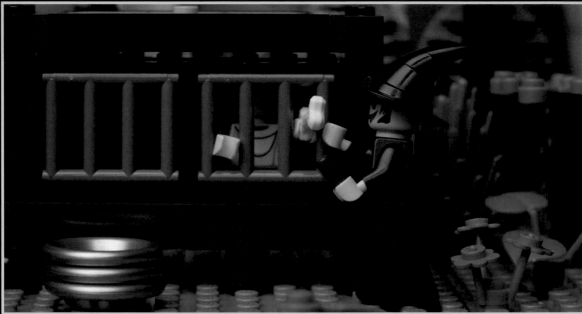

Hansel, however, stretched out a little bone to her, and the old woman, who had dim eyes, could not see it, and thought it was Hansel's finger, and was astonished that there was no way of fattening him.

When four weeks had gone by, and Hansel still continued thin, she was seized with impatience and would not wait any longer. "Hola, Gretel," she cried to the girl, "be active, and bring some water. Let Hansel be fat or lean, to-morrow I will kill him, and cook him."

Ah, how the poor little sister did lament when she had to fetch the water, and how her tears did flow down over her cheeks!

"Dear God, do help us," she cried. "If the wild beasts in the forest had but devoured us, we should at any rate have died together."

"Just keep thy noise to thyself," said the old woman, "all that won't help thee at all."

Early in the morning, Gretel had to go out and hang up the cauldron with the water, and light the fire.

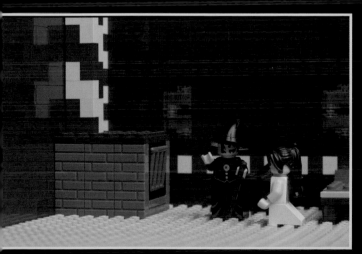

"We will bake first," said the old woman, "I have already heated the oven, and kneaded the dough."

She pushed poor Gretel out to the oven, from which flames of fire were already darting. "Creep in," said the witch, "and see if it is properly heated, so that we can shut the bread in."

And when once Gretel was inside, she intended to shut the oven and let her bake in it, and then she would eat her, too.

But Gretel saw what she had in her mind, and said, "I do not know how I am to do it; how do you get in?"

and she crept up and thrust her head into the oven.

"Silly goose," said the old woman, "The door is big enough; just look, I can get in myself!"

Then Gretel gave her a push that drove her far into it,

and shut the iron door, and fastened the bolt. Oh! then she began to howl quite horribly,

but Gretel ran away, and the godless witch was miserably burnt to death.

Gretel, however, ran like lightning to Hansel, opened his little stable, and cried, "Hansel, we are saved! The old witch is dead!"

Then Hansel sprang out like a bird from its cage when the door is opened for it. How they did rejoice and embrace each other, and dance about and kiss each other!

And as they had no longer any need to fear her, they went into the witch's house, and in every corner there stood chests full of pearls and jewels. "These are far better than pebbles!" said Hansel, and thrust into his pockets whatever could be got in,

and Gretel said, "I, too, will take something home with me," and filled her pinafore full. "But now we will go away," said Hansel, "that we may get out of the witch's forest."

When they had walked for two hours, they came to a great piece of water. "We cannot get over," said Hansel, "I see no foot-plank, and no bridge."

"And no boat crosses either," answered Gretel, "but a white duck is swimming there; if I ask her, she will help us over." Then she cried,

"Little duck, little duck, dost thou see,
Hansel and Gretel are waiting for thee?
There's never a plank, or bridge in sight,

Take us across on thy back so white."

The duck came to them, and Hansel seated himself on its back, and told his sister to sit by him.

"No," replied Gretel, "that will be too heavy for the little duck; she shall take us across, one after the other."

The good little duck did so,

and when they were once safely across and had walked for a short time, the forest seemed to be more and more familiar to them, and at length they saw from afar their father's house.

Then they began to run, rushed into the parlour,

and threw themselves into their father's arms.

The man had not known one happy hour since he had left the children in the forest; the woman, however, was dead.

Gretel emptied her pinafore until pearls and precious stones ran about the room, and Hansel threw one handful after another out of his pocket to add to them. Then all anxiety was at an end, and they lived together in perfect happiness.

My tale is done, there runs a mouse, whosoever catches it,

may make himself a big fur cap out of it.

The Frog-King

In old times when wishing still helped one, there lived a king whose daughters were all beautiful, but the youngest was so beautiful that the sun itself, which has seen so much, was astonished whenever it shone in her face.

Close by the King's castle lay a great dark forest, and under an old lime-tree in the forest was a well, and when the day was very warm, the King's child went out into the forest

and sat down by the side of the cool fountain, and when she was dull she took a golden ball,

and threw it up on high and caught it, and this ball was her favorite plaything.

Now it so happened that on one occasion the princess's golden ball did not fall into the little hand which she was holding up for it, but on to the ground beyond,

The King's daughter followed it with her eyes, but it vanished, and the well was deep, so deep that the bottom could not be seen.

and rolled straight into the water.

On this she began to cry, and cried louder and louder, and could not be comforted.

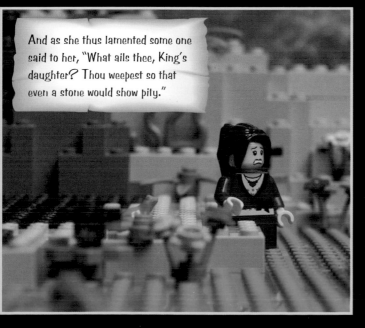

And as she thus lamented some one said to her, "What ails thee, King's daughter? Thou weepest so that even a stone would show pity."

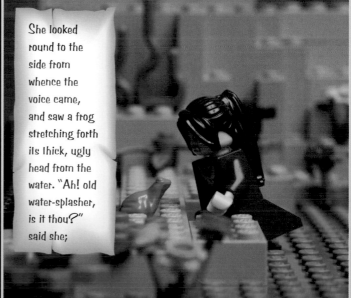

She looked round to the side from whence the voice came, and saw a frog stretching forth its thick, ugly head from the water. "Ah! old water-splasher, is it thou?" said she;

123

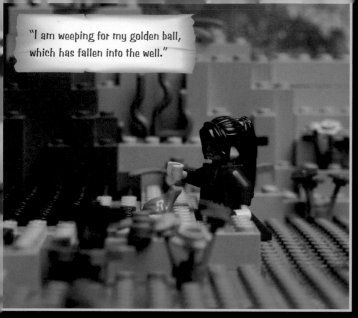

"I am weeping for my golden ball, which has fallen into the well."

"Be quiet, and do not weep," answered the frog, "I can help thee, but what wilt thou give me if I bring thy plaything up again?"

"Whatever thou wilt have, dear frog," said she— "My clothes, my pearls and jewels, and even the golden crown which I am wearing."

The frog answered, "I do not care for thy clothes, thy pearls and jewels, or thy golden crown, but if thou wilt love me and let me be thy companion and play-fellow,

and sit by thee at thy little table, and eat off thy little golden plate, and drink out of thy little cup,

and sleep in thy little bed—

if thou wilt promise me this I will go down below, and bring thee thy golden ball up again."

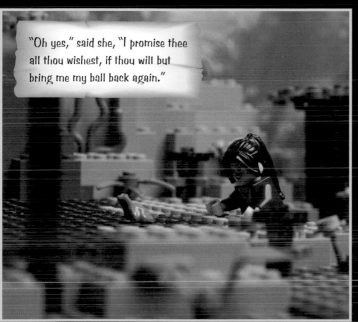

"Oh yes," said she, "I promise thee all thou wishest, if thou will but bring me my ball back again."

She, however, thought, "How the silly frog does talk! He lives in the water with the other frogs, and croaks, and can be no companion to any human being!"

But the frog when he had received this promise, put his head into the water and sank down, and in a short while came swimming up again with the ball in his mouth, and threw it on the grass.

The King's daughter was delighted to see her pretty plaything once more, and picked it up, and ran away with it.

"Wait, wait," said the frog. "Take me with thee. I can't run as thou canst." But what did it avail him to scream his croak, croak, after her, as loudly as he could?

She did not listen to it, but ran home and soon forgot the poor frog,

who was forced to go back into his well again.

The next day when she had seated herself at table with the King and all the courtiers, and was eating from her little golden plate,

something came creeping splish splash, splish splash, up the marble staircase, and when it had got to the top,

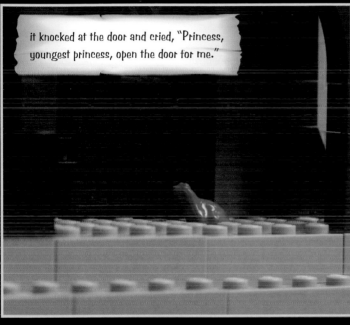

it knocked at the door and cried, "Princess, youngest princess, open the door for me."

She ran to see who was outside,

but when she opened the door, there sat the frog in front of it.

Then she slammed the door to, in great haste, sat down to dinner again, and was quite frightened.

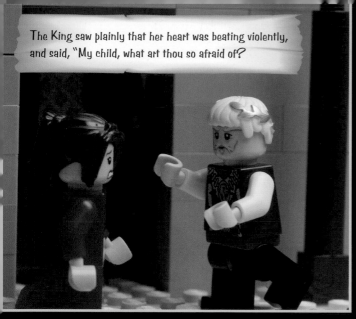

The King saw plainly that her heart was beating violently, and said, "My child, what art thou so afraid of?

Is there perchance a giant outside who wants to carry thee away?"

"Ah, no," replied she. "It is no giant but a disgusting frog."

"What does a frog want with thee?"

"Ah, dear father, yesterday as I was in the forest sitting by the well, playing, my golden ball fell into the water. And because I cried so, the frog brought it out again for me, and because he so insisted, I promised him he should be my companion, but I never thought he would be able to come out of his water! And now he is outside there, and wants to come in to me."

In the meantime it knocked a second time, and cried,

"Princess! youngest princess!
Open the door for me!
Dost thou not know what thou saidst to me

Yesterday by the cool waters of the fountain?
Princess, youngest princess!
Open the door for me!"

Then said the King, "That which thou hast promised must thou perform. Go and let him in."

She went and opened the door, and the frog hopped in and followed her, step by step, to her chair.

There he sat and cried, "Lift me up beside thee."

She delayed, until at last the King commanded her to do it.

When the frog was once on the chair he wanted to be on the table, and when he was on the table he said, "Now, push thy little golden plate nearer to me that we may eat together."

She did this, but it was easy to see that she did not do it willingly. The frog enjoyed what he ate, but almost every mouthful she took choked her.

At length he said, "I have eaten and am satisfied; now I am tired, carry me into thy little room and make thy little silken bed ready, and we will both lie down and go to sleep."

The King's daughter began to cry, for she was afraid of the cold frog which she did not like to touch, and which was now to sleep in her pretty, clean little bed.

But the King grew angry and said, "He who helped thee when thou wert in trouble ought not afterwards to be despised by thee."

So she took hold of the frog with two fingers, carried him upstairs,

and put him in a corner.

But when she was in bed

he crept to her and said, "I am tired, I want to sleep as well as thou, lift me up or I will tell thy father."

Then she was terribly angry, and took him up and threw him with all her might

against the wall.

"Now, thou wilt be quiet, odious frog," said she.

But when he fell down he was no frog but a King's son with beautiful kind eyes.

He by her father's will was now her dear companion and husband.

Then he told her how he had been bewitched by a wicked witch, and how no one could have delivered him from the well but herself,

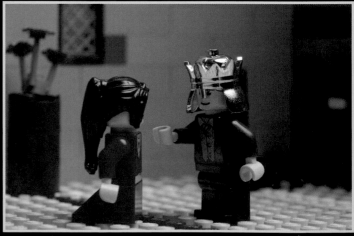

and that to-morrow they would go together into his kingdom.

Then they went to sleep,

and next morning when the sun awoke them, a carriage came driving up with eight white horses, which had white ostrich feathers on their heads, and were harnessed with golden chains, and behind stood the young King's servant Faithful Henry.

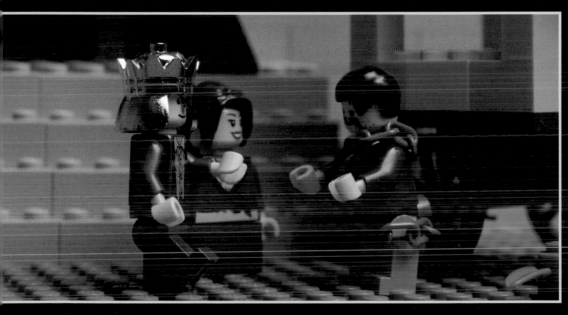

Faithful Henry had been so unhappy when his master was changed into a frog, that he had caused three iron bands to be laid round his heart, lest it should burst with grief and sadness.

The carriage was to conduct the young King into his Kingdom. Faithful Henry helped them both in, and placed himself behind again, and was full of joy because of this deliverance.

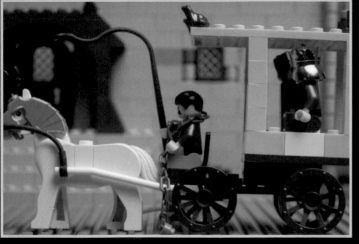

And when they had driven a part of the way the King's son heard a cracking behind him as if something had broken.

So he turned round and cried, "Henry, the carriage is breaking."

"No, master, it is not the carriage. It is a band from my heart, which was put there in my great pain when you were a frog and imprisoned in the well." Again and once again while they were on their way something cracked, and each time the King's son thought the carriage was breaking; but it was only the bands which were springing from the heart of faithful Henry because his master was set free and was happy.

Rumpelstiltskin

Once there was a miller who was poor, but who had a beautiful daughter. Now it happened that he had to go and speak to the King,

and in order to make himself appear important he said to him, "I have a daughter who can spin straw into gold."

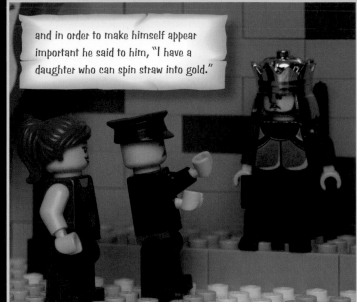

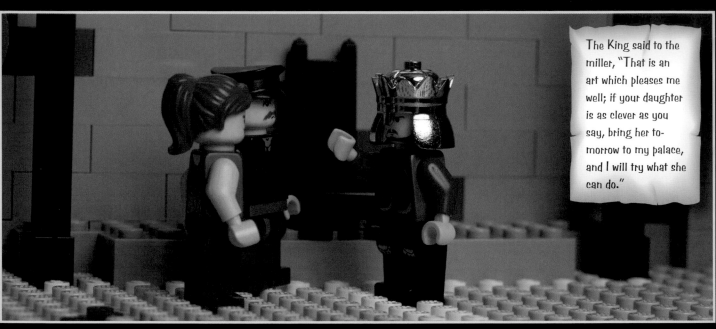

The King said to the miller, "That is an art which pleases me well; if your daughter is as clever as you say, bring her to-morrow to my palace, and I will try what she can do."

And when the girl was brought to him he took her into a room which was quite full of straw, gave her a spinning-wheel and a reel,

and said, "Now set to work, and if by to-morrow morning early you have not spun this straw into gold during the night, you must die." Thereupon he himself locked up the room, and left her in it alone.

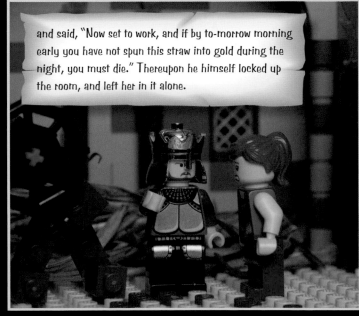

So there sat the poor miller's daughter, and for the life of her could not tell what to do; she had no idea how straw could be spun into gold, and she grew more and more miserable, until at last she began to weep.

But all at once the door opened, and in came a little man, and said, "Good evening, Mistress Miller; why are you crying so?"

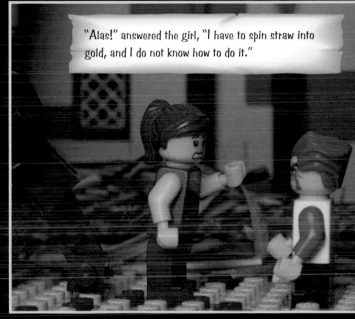

"Alas!" answered the girl, "I have to spin straw into gold, and I do not know how to do it."

"What will you give me," said the manikin, "if I do it for you?"

"My necklace," said the girl. The little man took the necklace, seated himself in front of the wheel,

and "whirr, whirr, whirr," three turns, and the reel was full; then he put another on, and whirr, whirr, whirr, three times round, and the second was full too. And so it went on until the morning, when all the straw was spun, and all the reels were full of gold.

By daybreak the King was already there, and when he saw the gold he was astonished and delighted, but his heart became only more greedy.

He had the miller's daughter taken into another room full of straw, which was much larger, and commanded her to spin that also in one night if she valued her life.

The girl knew not how to help herself, and was crying,

when the door again opened, and the little man appeared, and said, "What will you give me if I spin that straw into gold for you?"

"The ring on my finger," answered the girl.

The little man took the ring, again began to turn the wheel, and by morning had spun all the straw into glittering gold.

The King rejoiced beyond measure at the sight,

but still he had not gold enough;

and he had the miller's daughter taken into a still larger room full of straw,

and said, "You must spin this, too, in the course of this night; but if you succeed, you shall be my wife."

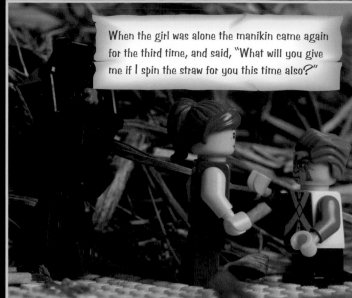

When the girl was alone the manikin came again for the third time, and said, "What will you give me if I spin the straw for you this time also?"

"Even if she be a miller's daughter," thought he, "I could not find a richer wife in the whole world."

"I have nothing left that I could give," answered the girl.

"Then promise me, if you should become Queen, your first child."

"Who knows whether that will ever happen?" thought the miller's daughter;

and for that he once more span the straw into gold.

and, not knowing how else to help herself in this strait, she promised the manikin what he wanted,

And when the King came in the morning, and found all as he had wished, he took her in marriage, and the pretty miller's daughter became a Queen.

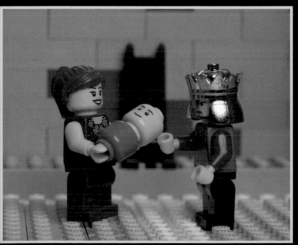

A year after, she had a beautiful child, and she never gave a thought to the manikin.

But suddenly he came into her room, and said, "Now give me what you promised." The Queen was horror-struck,

and offered the manikin all the riches of the kingdom if he would leave her the child.

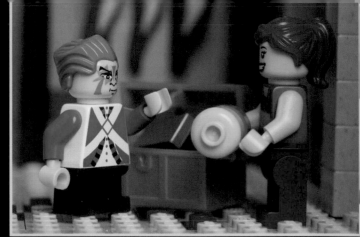

But the manikin said, "No, something that is living is dearer to me than all the treasures in the world."

Then the Queen began to weep and cry, so that the manikin pitied her.

"I will give you three days' time," said he, "if by that time you find out my name, then shall you keep your child."

So the Queen thought the whole night of all the names that she had ever heard,

and she sent a messenger over the country to inquire, far and wide, for any other names that there might be.

When the manikin came the next day, she began with Caspar, Melchior, Balthazar, and said all the names she knew, one after another;

but to every one the little man said, "That is not my name."

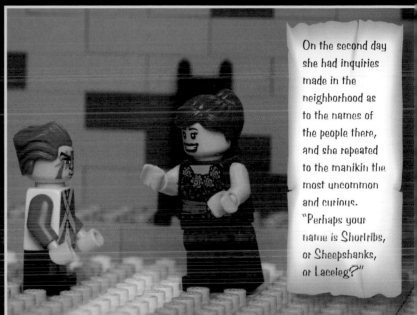

On the second day she had inquiries made in the neighborhood as to the names of the people there, and she repeated to the manikin the most uncommon and curious. "Perhaps your name is Shortribs, or Sheepshanks, or Laceleg?"

but he always answered, "That is not my name."

On the third day the messenger came back again, and said, "I have not been able to find a single new name,

but as I came to a high mountain at the end of the forest, where the fox and the hare bid each other good night, there I saw a little house, and before the house a fire was burning,

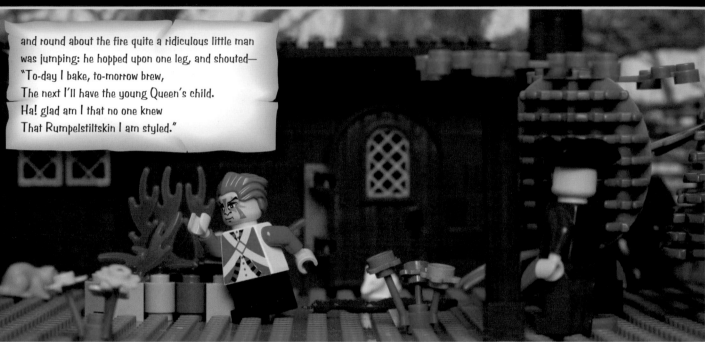

and round about the fire quite a ridiculous little man was jumping: he hopped upon one leg, and shouted—
"To-day I bake, to-morrow brew,
The next I'll have the young Queen's child.
Ha! glad am I that no one knew
That Rumpelstiltskin I am styled."

You may think how glad the Queen was when she heard the name!

And when soon afterwards the little man came in, and asked, "Now, Mistress Queen, what is my name?"

at first she said, "Is your name Conrad?" "No."

"Is your name Harry?" "No."

"Perhaps your name is Rumpelstiltskin?"

"The devil has told you that! The devil has told you that!" cried the little man,

and in his anger he plunged his right foot so deep into the earth that his whole leg went in;

and then in rage he pulled at his left leg so hard with both hands

that he tore himself in two.

Little Red Riding Hood

Once upon a time there was a dear little girl who was loved by every one who looked at her, but most of all by her grandmother, and there was nothing that she would not have given to the child.

Once she gave her a little cap of red velvet, which suited her so well that she would never wear anything else; so she was always called "Little Red-Cap."

One day her mother said to her, "Come, Little Red-Cap, here is a piece of cake and a bottle of wine; take them to your grandmother, she is ill and weak, and they will do her good.

Set out before it gets hot, and when you are going, walk nicely and quietly

and do not run off the path, or you may fall and break the bottle, and then your grandmother will get nothing; and when you go into her room, don't forget to say, 'Good-morning,' and don't peep into every corner before you do it."

The grandmother lived out in the wood, half a league from the village, and just as Little Red-Cap entered the wood, a wolf met her. Red-Cap did not know what a wicked creature he was, and was not at all afraid of him.

"Good-day, Little Red-Cap," said he.

"Thank you kindly, wolf."

"Whither away so early, Little Red-Cap?"

"To my grandmother's."

"What have you got in your apron?"

"Cake and wine; yesterday was baking-day, so poor sick grandmother is to have something good, to make her stronger."

"Where does your grandmother live, Little Red-Cap?"

"A good quarter of a league farther on in the wood; her house stands under the three large oak-trees, the nut-trees are just below; you surely must know it," replied Little Red-Cap.

The wolf thought to himself, "What a tender young creature! what a nice plump mouthful—she will be better to eat than the old woman. I must act craftily, so as to catch both."

So he walked for a short time by the side of Little Red-Cap, and then he said, "See Little Red-Cap, how pretty the flowers are about here—why do you not look round? I believe, too, that you do not hear how sweetly the little birds are singing; you walk gravely along as if you were going to school, while everything else out here in the wood is merry."

Little Red-Cap raised her eyes, and when she saw the sunbeams dancing here and there through the trees, and pretty flowers growing everywhere, she thought, "Suppose I take grandmother a fresh nosegay; that would please her too. It is so early in the day that I shall still get there in good time;"

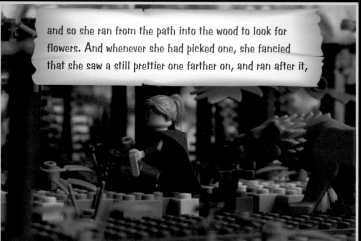

and so she ran from the path into the wood to look for flowers. And whenever she had picked one, she fancied that she saw a still prettier one farther on, and ran after it,

and so got deeper and deeper into the wood.

Meanwhile the wolf ran straight to the grandmother's house

and knocked at the door.

"Who is there?"

"Little Red-Cap," replied the wolf. "She is bringing cake and wine; open the door."

"Lift the latch," called out the grandmother, "I am too weak, and cannot get up."

The wolf lifted the latch, the door flew open,

and without saying a word he went straight to the grandmother's bed, and devoured her.

Then he put on her clothes, dressed himself in her cap,

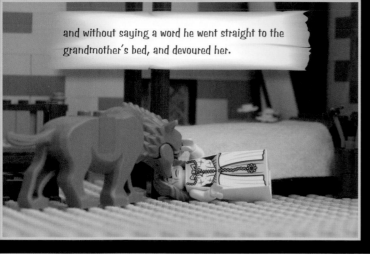

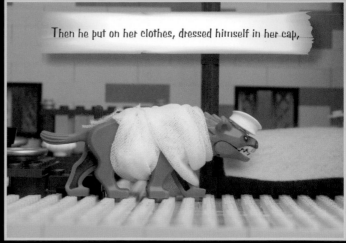

laid himself in bed and drew the curtains.

Little Red-Cap, however, had been running about picking flowers, and when she had gathered so many that she could carry no more, she remembered her grandmother, and set out on the way to her.

She was surprised to find the cottage-door standing open,

and when she went into the room, she had such a strange feeling that she said to herself, "Oh dear! how uneasy I feel to-day, and at other times I like being with grandmother so much."

She called out, "Good morning," but received no answer; so she went to the bed and drew back the curtains.

There lay her grandmother with her cap pulled far over her face, and looking very strange.

"Oh! grandmother," she said, "what big ears you have!"

"The better to hear you with, my child," was the reply.

"But, grandmother, what big eyes you have!" she said.

"The better to see you with, my dear."

"But, grandmother, what large hands you have!"

"The better to hug you with."

"Oh! but, grandmother, what a terrible big mouth you have!"

"The better to eat you with!"

And scarcely had the wolf said this, than with one bound he was out of bed and swallowed up Red-Cap.

When the wolf had appeased his appetite, he lay down again near the bed, fell asleep and began to snore very loud.

The huntsman was just passing the house, and thought to himself, "How the old woman is snoring! I must just see if she wants anything."

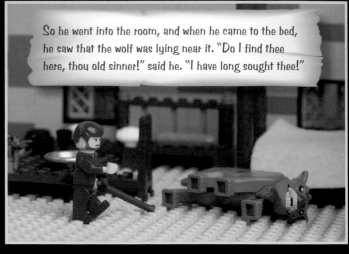

So he went into the room, and when he came to the bed, he saw that the wolf was lying near it. "Do I find thee here, thou old sinner!" said he. "I have long sought thee!"

Then just as he was going to fire at him, it occurred to him that the wolf might have devoured the grandmother, and that she might still be saved, so he did not fire,

but took a pair of scissors, and began to cut open the stomach of the sleeping wolf.

When he had made two snips, he saw the little Red-Cap shining, and then he made two snips more,

and the little girl sprang out, crying, "Ah, how frightened I have been! How dark it was inside the wolf;"

and after that the aged grandmother came out alive also, but scarcely able to breathe.

with which they filled the wolf's body,

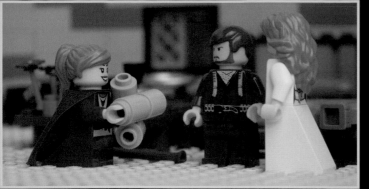

Red-Cap, however, quickly fetched great stones

and when he awoke, he wanted to run away,

but the stones were so heavy that he fell down at once, and fell dead.

Then all three were delighted. The huntsman drew off the wolf's skin and went home with it;

the grandmother ate the cake and drank the wine which Red-Cap had brought, and revived,

but Red-Cap thought to herself, "As long as I live, I will never by myself leave the path, to run into the wood, when my mother has forbidden me to do so."

It is also related that once when Red-Cap was again taking cakes to the old grandmother, another wolf spoke to her, and tried to entice her from the path.

Red-Cap, however, was on her guard, and went straight forward on her way,

"Well," said the grandmother, "we will shut the door, that he may not come in."

and told her grandmother that she had met the wolf, and that he had said "good-morning" to her, but with such a wicked look in his eyes, that if they had not been on the public road she was certain he would have eaten her up.

Soon afterwards the wolf knocked, and cried, "Open the door, grandmother, I am little Red-Cap, and am fetching you some cakes."

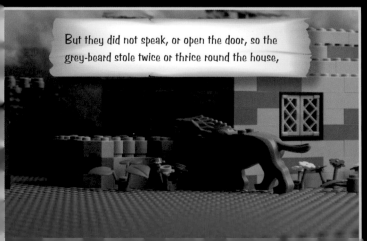

But they did not speak, or open the door, so the grey-beard stole twice or thrice round the house,

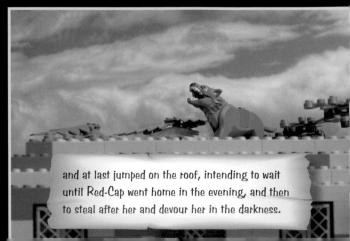

and at last jumped on the roof, intending to wait until Red-Cap went home in the evening, and then to steal after her and devour her in the darkness.

But the grandmother saw what was in his thoughts. In front of the house was a great stone trough, so she said to the child, "Take the pail, Red-Cap; I made some sausages yesterday, so carry the water in which I boiled them to the trough."

Red-Cap carried until the great trough was quite full.

Then the smell of the sausages reached the wolf, and he sniffed and peeped down,

and at last stretched out his neck so far that he could no longer keep his footing and began to slip,

and slipped down from the roof straight into the great trough,

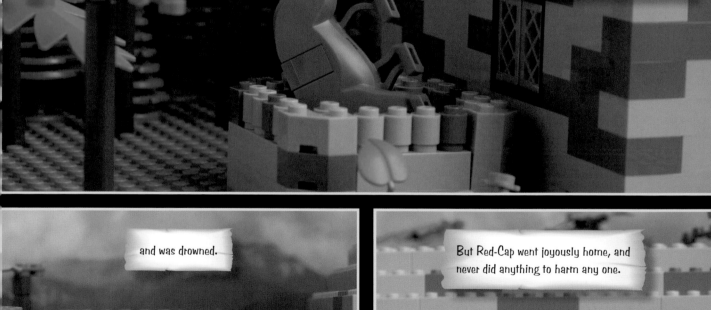

and was drowned.

But Red-Cap went joyously home, and never did anything to harm any one.

Little Briar-Rose (Sleeping Beauty)

A long time ago there were a King and Queen who said every day, "Ah, if only we had a child!" but they never had one.

But it happened that once when the Queen was bathing, a frog crept out of the water on to the land, and said to her, "Your wish shall be fulfilled; before a year has gone by, you shall have a daughter."

What the frog had said came true, and the Queen had a little girl who was so pretty that the King could not contain himself for joy, and ordered a great feast. He invited not only his kindred, friends and acquaintance, but also the Wise Women, in order that they might be kind and well-disposed towards the child. There were thirteen of them in his kingdom, but, as he had only twelve golden plates for them to eat out of, one of them had to be left at home.

The feast was held with all manner of splendour and when it came to an end the Wise Women bestowed their magic gifts upon the baby: one gave virtue, another beauty, a third riches, and so on with everything in the world that one can wish for.

When eleven of them had made their promises, suddenly the thirteenth came in. She wished to avenge herself for not having been invited, and without greeting, or even looking at any one, she cried with a loud voice, "The King's daughter shall in her fifteenth year prick herself with a spindle, and fall down dead." And, without saying a word more, she turned round and left the room.

They were all shocked; but the twelfth, whose good wish still remained unspoken, came forward, and as she could not undo the evil sentence, but only soften it, she said, "It shall not be death, but a deep sleep of a hundred years, into which the princess shall fall."

The King, who would fain keep his dear child from the misfortune, gave orders that every spindle in the whole kingdom should be burnt.

Meanwhile the gifts of the Wise Women were plenteously fulfilled on the young girl, for she was so beautiful, modest, good-natured, and wise, that everyone who saw her was bound to love her.

It happened that on the very day when she was fifteen years old, the King and Queen were not at home, and the maiden was left in the palace quite alone. So she went round into all sorts of places, looked into rooms and bed-chambers just as she liked, and at last came to an old tower.

She climbed up the narrow winding-staircase,

and reached a little door. A rusty key was in the lock, and when she turned it the door sprang open,

and there in a little room sat an old woman with a spindle, busily spinning her flax.

"Good day, old dame," said the King's daughter; "what are you doing there?"

"I am spinning," said the old woman, and nodded her head.

"What sort of thing is that, that rattles round so merrily?" said the girl,

and she took the spindle and wanted to spin too. But scarcely had she touched the spindle when the magic decree was fulfilled, and she pricked her finger with it.

And, in the very moment when she felt the prick, she fell down upon the bed that stood there, and lay in a deep sleep.

And this sleep extended over the whole palace; the King and Queen, who had just come home, and had entered the great hall, began to go to sleep, and the whole of the court with them.

The horses, too, went to sleep in the stable,

the dogs in the yard, the pigeons upon the roof, the flies on the wall;

even the fire that was flaming on the hearth became quiet and slept, the roast meat left off frizzling, and the cook, who was just going to pull the hair of the scullery boy, because he had forgotten something, let him go, and went to sleep.

And the wind fell, and on the trees before the castle not a leaf moved again.

But round about the castle there began to grow a hedge of thorns, which every year became higher,

and at last grew close up round the castle and all over it, so that there was nothing of it to be seen, not even the flag upon the roof.

But the story of the beautiful sleeping "Briar-rose," for so the princess was named, went about the country, so that from time to time kings' sons came and tried to get through the thorny hedge into the castle.

But they found it impossible, for the thorns held fast together, as if they had hands, and the youths were caught in them, could not get loose again, and died a miserable death.

After long, long years a King's son came again to that country, and heard an old man talking about the thorn-hedge, and that a castle was said to stand behind it in which a wonderfully beautiful princess, named Briar-rose, had been asleep for a hundred years; and that the King and Queen and the whole court were asleep likewise.

He had heard, too, from his grandfather, that many kings' sons had already come, and had tried to get through the thorny hedge, but they had remained sticking fast in it, and had died a pitiful death. Then the youth said, "I am not afraid, I will go and see the beautiful Briar-rose." The good old man might dissuade him as he would, he did not listen to his words.

But by this time the hundred years had just passed, and the day had come when Briar-rose was to awake again. When the King's son came near to the thorn-hedge, it was nothing but large and beautiful flowers, which parted from each other of their own accord, and let him pass unhurt, then they closed again behind him like a hedge.

In the castle-yard he saw the horses and the spotted hounds lying asleep; on the roof sat the pigeons with their heads under their wings.

And when he entered the house, the flies were asleep upon the wall, the cook in the kitchen was still holding out his hand to seize the boy, and the maid was sitting by the black hen which she was going to pluck.

He went on farther, and in the great hall he saw the whole of the court lying asleep, and up by the throne lay the King and Queen.

Then he went on still farther, and all was so quiet that a breath could be heard, and at last he came to the tower,

and opened the door into the little room where Briar-rose was sleeping.

There she lay, so beautiful that he could not turn his eyes away;

and he stooped down and gave her a kiss.

But as soon as he kissed her, Briar-rose opened her eyes and awoke, and looked at him quite sweetly.

Then they went down together,

and the King awoke, and the Queen, and the whole court, and looked at each other in great astonishment.

And the horses in the court-yard stood up and shook themselves; the hounds jumped up and wagged their tails; the pigeons upon the roof pulled out their heads from under their wings, looked round, and flew into the open country; the flies on the wall crept again;

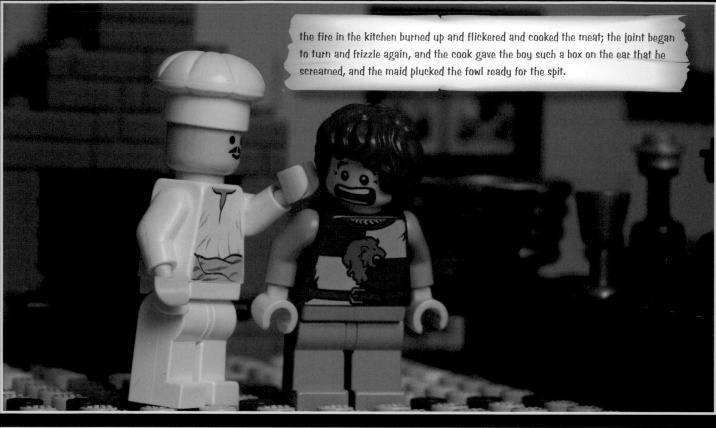

the fire in the kitchen burned up and flickered and cooked the meat; the joint began to turn and frizzle again, and the cook gave the boy such a box on the ear that he screamed, and the maid plucked the fowl ready for the spit.

And then the marriage of the King's son with Briar-rose was celebrated with all splendour, and they lived contented to the end of their days.

Clever Hans

Hans comes to Grethel, "Good day, Grethel." "Good day, Hans. What dost thou bring that is good?"

The mother of Hans said, "Whither away, Hans?" Hans answered, "To Grethel." "Behave well, Hans." "Oh, I'll behave well. Good-bye, mother." "Good-bye, Hans."

"I bring nothing, I want to have something given me."

Grethel presents Hans with a needle.

Hans says, "Good-bye, Grethel." "Good-bye, Hans."

Hans takes the needle, sticks it into a hay-cart, and follows the cart home.

"Good evening, mother." "Good evening, Hans. Where hast thou been?"

"With Grethel."

179

"What didst thou take her?"

"Took nothing; had something given me."

"What did Grethel give thee?" "Gave me a needle."

"Where is the needle, Hans?"

"Good day, Grethel."

"Good day, Hans. What dost thou bring that is good?"

"I bring nothing; I want to have something given to me."

Grethel presents Hans with a knife.

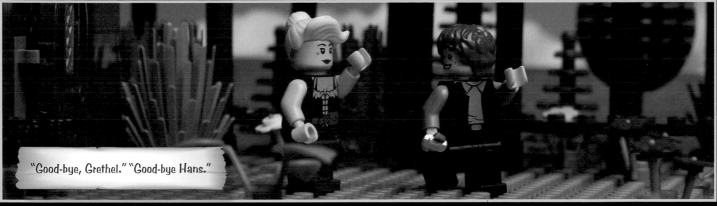

"Good-bye, Grethel." "Good-bye Hans."

Hans takes the knife, sticks it in his sleeve, and goes home.

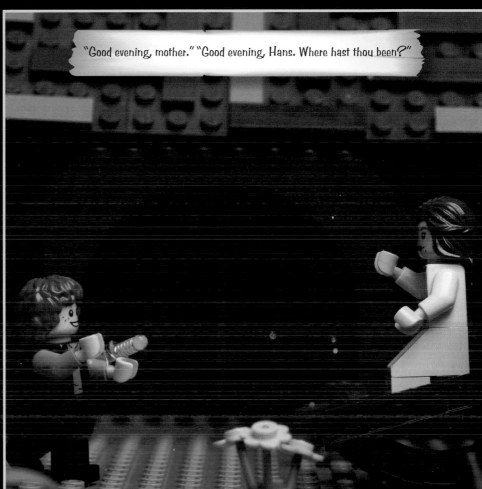

"Good evening, mother." "Good evening, Hans. Where hast thou been?"

"With Grethel."

"What didst thou take her?"

"Whither away, Hans?" "To Grethel, mother." "Behave well, Hans." "Oh, I'll behave well. Good-bye, mother." "Good-bye, Hans."

Hans comes to Grethel. "Good day, Grethel." "Good day, Hans. What good thing dost thou bring?"

"I bring nothing, I want something given me."

Grethel presents Hans with a young goat.

"Good-bye, Grethel." "Good-bye, Hans."

185

Hans takes the goat,

ties its legs, and puts it in his pocket.

When he gets home it is suffocated. "Good evening, mother." "Good evening, Hans. Where hast thou been?"

"Put it in my pocket."

"That was ill done, Hans, thou shouldst have put a rope round the goat's neck."

"Never mind, will do better next time."

"Whither away, Hans?" "To Grethel, mother." "Behave well, Hans." "Oh, I'll behave well. Good-bye, mother." "Good-bye, Hans."

Hans comes to Grethel. "Good day, Grethel." "Good day, Hans. What good thing dost thou bring?"

"I bring nothing, I want something given me."

Grethel presents Hans with a piece of bacon.

"Good-bye, Grethel." "Good-bye, Hans."

Hans takes the bacon, ties it to a rope, and drags it away behind him.

The dogs come and devour the bacon. When he gets home, he has the rope in his hand, and there is no longer anything hanging to it.

"Good evening, mother." "Good evening, Hans."

"Where hast thou been?" "With Grethel."

"What didst thou take her?"

"I took her nothing, she gave me something."

"Whither away, Hans?" "To Grethel, mother." "Behave well, Hans." "I'll behave well. Good-bye, mother." "Good-bye, Hans."

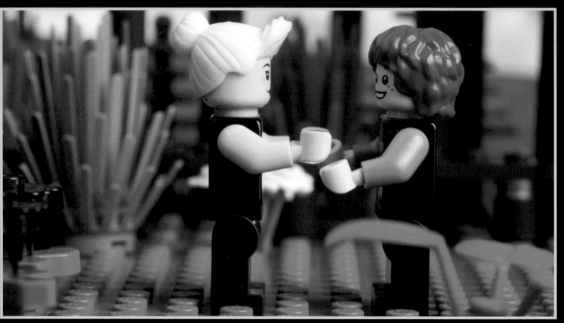

Hans comes to Grethel. "Good day, Grethel." "Good day, Hans." "What good thing dost thou bring?"

"I bring nothing, but would have something given."

Grethel presents Hans with a calf.

"Good-bye, Grethel." "Good-bye, Hans."

Hans takes the calf, puts it on his head,

and the calf kicks his face.

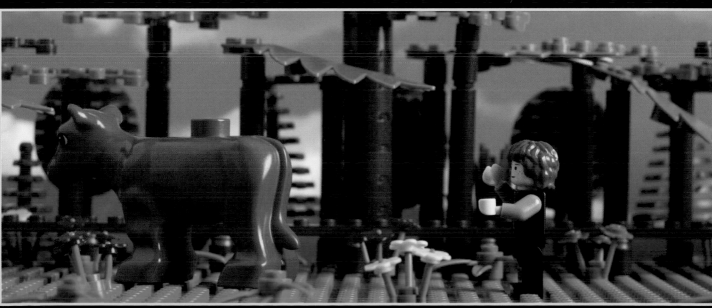

"I bring nothing, but would have something given."

Grethel says to Hans, "I will go with thee."

Hans takes Grethel, ties her to a rope,

leads her to the rack,

and binds her fast.

Then Hans goes to his mother. "Good evening, mother." "Good evening, Hans. Where hast thou been?"

"With Grethel."

"What didst thou take her?"

"I took her nothing."

"What did Grethel give thee?" "She gave me nothing, she came with me."

"Where hast thou left Grethel?"

"I led her by the rope, tied her to the rack, and scattered some grass for her."

"That was ill done, Hans, thou shouldst have cast friendly eyes on her."

"Never mind, will do better."

Hans went into the stable,

cut out all the calves' and sheeps' eyes,

and threw them in Grethel's face.

Then Grethel became angry,

tore herself loose and ran away,

and became the bride of Hans.

A poor man had twelve children and was forced to work night and day to give them even bread.

When therefore the thirteenth came into the world, he knew not what to do in his trouble,

but ran out into the great highway, and resolved to ask the first person whom he met to be godfather.

The first to meet him was the good God who already knew what filled his heart,

and said to him, "Poor man, I pity thee. I will hold thy child at its christening, and will take charge of it and make it happy on earth."

The man said, "Who art thou?"

"I am God."

"Then I do not desire to have thee for a godfather," said the man;

"thou givest to the rich, and leavest the poor to hunger."

Thus spoke the man, for he did not know how wisely God apportions riches and poverty. He turned therefore away from the Lord, and went farther.

Then the Devil came to him and said, "What seekest thou?

If thou wilt take me as a godfather for thy child, I will give him gold in plenty and all the joys of the world as well."

The man asked, "Who art thou?" "I am the Devil."

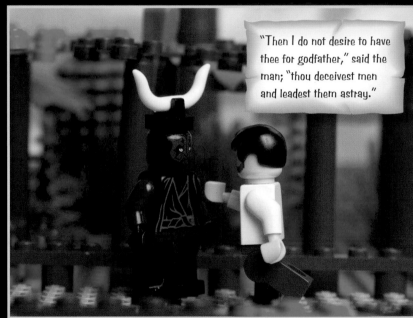

"Then I do not desire to have thee for godfather," said the man; "thou deceivest men and leadest them astray."

He went onwards,

and then came Death striding up to him with withered legs,

and said, "Take me as godfather."

The man asked, "Who art thou?"

"I am Death, and I make all equal."

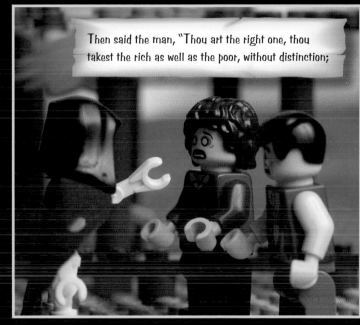

Then said the man, "Thou art the right one, thou takest the rich as well as the poor, without distinction;

thou shalt be godfather."

Death answered, "I will make thy child rich and famous, for he who has me for a friend can lack nothing."

The man said, "Next Sunday is the christening; be there at the right time."

Death appeared as he had promised, and stood godfather quite in the usual way.

When the boy had grown up, his godfather one day appeared and bade him go with him.

He led him forth into a forest, and showed him a herb which grew there,

and said, "Now shalt thou receive thy godfather's present. I make thee a celebrated physician.

When thou art called to a patient, I will always appear to thee. If I stand by the head of the sick man, thou mayst say with confidence that thou wilt make him well again,

and if thou givest him of this herb

he will recover;

but if I stand by the patient's feet,

he is mine, and thou must say that all remedies are in vain,

and that no physician in the world could save him.

But beware of using the herb against my will, or it might fare ill with thee."

It was not long before the youth was the most famous physician in the whole world. "He had only to look at the patient and he knew his condition at once, and if he would recover, or must needs die." So they said of him, and from far and wide people came to him, sent for him when they had any one ill, and gave him so much money that he soon became a rich man.

Now it so befell that the King became ill, and the physician was summoned, and was to say if recovery were possible.

But when he came to the bed, Death was standing by the feet of the sick man, and the herb did not grow which could save him.

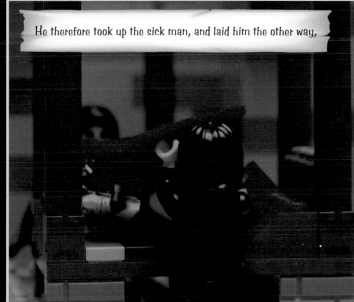

"If I could but cheat Death for once," thought the physician, "he is sure to take it ill if I do, but, as I am his godson, he will shut one eye; I will risk it."

He therefore took up the sick man, and laid him the other way, so that now Death was standing by his head. Then he gave the King some of the herb,

and he recovered and grew healthy again.

But Death came to the physician, looking very black and angry, threatened him with his finger, and said, "Thou hast overreached me; this time I will pardon it, as thou art my godson; but if thou venturest it again, it will cost thee thy neck, for I will take thee thyself away with me."

Soon afterwards the King's daughter fell into a severe illness. She was his only child, and he wept day and night, so that he began to lose the sight of his eyes,

and he caused it to be made known that whosoever rescued her from death should be her husband and inherit the crown.

When the physician came to the sick girl's bed, he saw Death by her feet. He ought to have remembered the warning given by his godfather, but he was so infatuated by the great beauty of the King's daughter, and the happiness of becoming her husband, that he flung all thought to the winds.

He did not see that Death was casting angry glances on him, that he was raising his hand in the air, and threatening him with his withered fist.

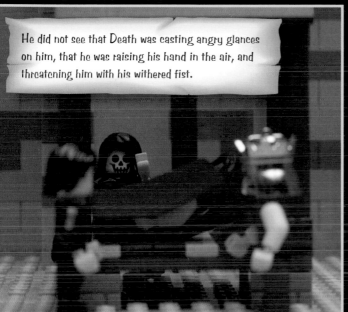

He raised up the sick girl, and placed her head where her feet had lain.

Then he gave her some of the herb,

and instantly her cheeks flushed red, and life stirred afresh in her.

and said, "All is over with thee, and now the lot falls on thee,"

When Death saw that for a second time he was defrauded of his own property, he walked up to the physician with long strides,

and seized him so firmly with his ice-cold hand, that he could not resist,

and led him into a cave below the earth.

There he saw how thousands and thousands of candles were burning in countless rows, some large, others half-sized, others small. Every instant some were extinguished, and others again burnt up, so that the flames seemed to leap hither and thither in perpetual change.

"See," said Death, "these are the lights of men's lives.

The large ones belong to children,

the half-sized ones to married people in their prime,

the little ones belong to old people; but children and young folks likewise have often only a tiny candle."

"Show me the light of my life," said the physician, and he thought that it would be still very tall.

Death pointed to a little end which was just threatening to go out, and said, "Behold, it is there."

"I cannot," answered Death, "one must go out before a new one is lighted."

"Ah, dear godfather," said the horrified physician, "light a new one for me, do it for love of me, that I may enjoy my life, be King, and the husband of the King's beautiful daughter."

"Then place the old one on a new one, that will go on burning at once when the old one has come to an end," pleaded the physician.

Death behaved as if he were going to fulfill his wish, and took hold of a tall new candle;

but as he desired to revenge himself, he purposely made a mistake in fixing it,

and the little piece fell down and was extinguished.

Immediately the physician fell on the ground,

and now he himself was in the hands of Death.

Sweet Porridge

So the child went into the forest,

There was a poor but good little girl who lived alone with her mother, and they no longer had anything to eat.

and there an aged woman met her who was aware of her sorrow, and presented her with a little pot,

which when she said, "Cook, little pot, cook," would cook good, sweet porridge,

and when she said, "Stop, little pot,"

it ceased to cook.

The girl took the pot home to her mother, and now they were freed from their poverty and hunger, and ate sweet porridge as often as they chose.

Once on a time when the girl had gone out,

her mother said, "Cook, little pot, cook."

And it did cook and she ate till she was satisfied,

and then she wanted the pot to stop cooking, but did not know the word.

So it went on cooking and the porridge rose over the edge,

and still it cooked on until the kitchen

and whole house were full,

and then the next house,

219

and then the whole street, just as if it wanted to satisfy the hunger of the whole world, and there was the greatest distress, but no one knew how to stop it.

At last when only one single house remained, the child came home and just said, "Stop, little pot," and it stopped and gave up cooking,

and whosoever wished to return to the town had to eat his way back.

The Shoes That Were Danced to Pieces

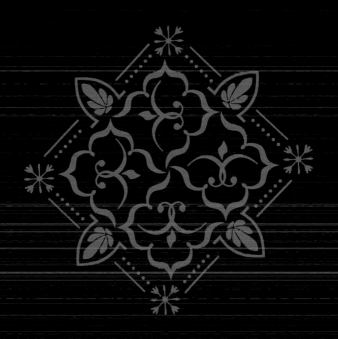

There was once upon a time a King who had twelve daughters, each one more beautiful than the other.

They all slept together in one chamber, in which their beds stood side by side,

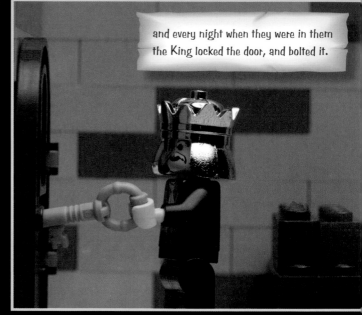

and every night when they were in them the King locked the door, and bolted it.

But in the morning when he unlocked the door, he saw that their shoes were worn out with dancing, and no one could find out how that had come to pass.

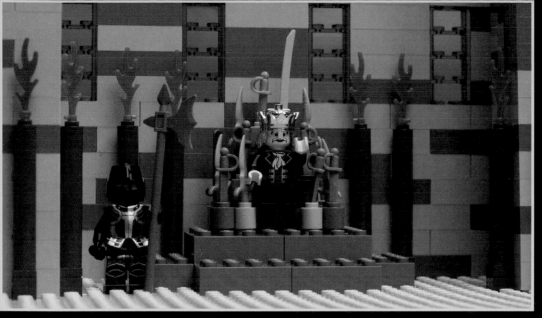

Then the King caused it to be proclaimed that whosoever could discover where they danced at night, should choose one of them for his wife and be King after his death, but that whosoever came forward and had not discovered it within three days and nights, should have forfeited his life.

It was not long before a King's son presented himself, and offered to undertake the enterprise.

He was well received,

and in the evening was led into a room adjoining the princesses' sleeping-chamber.

His bed was placed there, and he was to observe where they went and danced, and in order that they might do nothing secretly or go away to some other place, the door of their room was left open.

223

But the eyelids of the prince grew heavy as lead, and he fell asleep,

and when he awoke in the morning, all twelve had been to the dance, for their shoes were standing there with holes in the soles.

Many others came after this and undertook the enterprise,

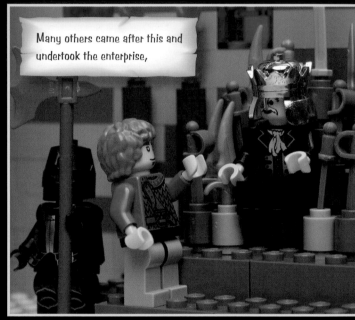

On the second and third nights it fell out just the same, and then his head was struck off without mercy.

but all forfeited their lives.

Now it came to pass that a poor soldier, who had a wound, and could serve no longer, found himself on the road to the town where the King lived.

There he met an old woman, who asked him where he was going. "I hardly know myself," answered he,

and added in jest, "I had half a mind to discover where the princesses danced their shoes into holes, and thus become King."

"That is not so difficult," said the old woman,

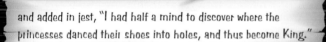

"you must not drink the wine which will be brought to you at night, and must pretend to be sound asleep."

With that she gave him a little cloak, and said, "If you put on that, you will be invisible, and then you can steal after the twelve."

When the soldier had received this good advice, he went into the thing in earnest, took heart,

went to the King, and announced himself as a suitor.

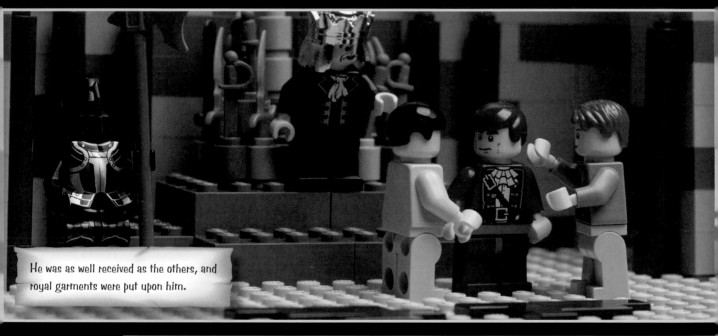

He was as well received as the others, and royal garments were put upon him.

He was conducted that evening at bed-time into the ante-chamber, and as he was about to go to bed, the eldest came and brought him a cup of wine, but he had tied a sponge under his chin,

and let the wine run down into it, without drinking a drop.

Then he lay down and when he had lain a while, he began to snore, as if in the deepest sleep. The twelve princesses heard that, and laughed.

and the eldest said, "He, too, might as well have saved his life."

dressed themselves before the mirrors,

With that they got up, opened wardrobes, presses, cupboards, and brought out pretty dresses;

sprang about, and rejoiced at the prospect of the dance.

Only the youngest said, "I know not how it is; you are very happy, but I feel very strange; some misfortune is certainly about to befall us."

"Thou art a goose, who art always frightened," said the eldest. "Hast thou forgotten how many Kings' sons have already come here in vain?

I had hardly any need to give the soldier a sleeping-draught, in any case the clown would not have awakened."

When they were all ready they looked carefully at the soldier, but he had closed his eyes and did not move or stir, so they felt themselves quite secure.

The eldest then went to her bed and tapped it;

it immediately sank into the earth,

229

and one after the other they descended through the opening, the eldest going first.

The soldier, who had watched everything, tarried no longer,

put on his little cloak,

and went down last with the youngest.

Half-way down the steps, he just trod a little on her dress;

she was terrified at that,

and cried out, "What is that? who is pulling my dress?"

"Don't be so silly!" said the eldest, "you have caught it on a nail."

Then they went all the way down, and when they were at the bottom, they were standing in a wonderfully pretty avenue of trees, all the leaves of which were of silver, and shone and glistened.

The soldier thought, "I must carry a token away with me,"

and broke off a twig from one of them, on which the tree cracked with a loud report.

The youngest cried out again. "Something is wrong, did you hear the crack?"

But the eldest said, "It is a gun fired for joy, because we have got rid of our prince so quickly."

After that they came into an avenue where all the leaves were of gold,

and lastly into a third where they were of bright diamonds;

he broke off a twig from each,

which made such a crack each time that the youngest started back in terror, but the eldest still maintained that they were salutes.

They went on and came to a great lake whereon stood twelve little boats, and in every boat sat a handsome prince, all of whom were waiting for the twelve, and each took one of them with him,

but the soldier seated himself by the youngest.

Then her prince said, "I can't tell why the boat is so much heavier to-day; I shall have to row with all my strength, if I am to get it across."

"What should cause that," said the youngest, "but the warm weather? I feel very warm too."

On the opposite side of the lake stood a splendid, brightly lit castle, from whence resounded the joyous music of trumpets and kettle-drums.

They rowed over there, entered, and each prince danced with the girl he loved,

but the soldier danced with them unseen,

and when one of them had a cup of wine in her hand he drank it up,

the youngest was alarmed at this,

so that the cup was empty when she carried it to her mouth;

but the eldest always made her be silent.

They danced there till three o'clock in the morning when all the shoes were danced into holes, and they were forced to leave off;

the princes rowed them back again over the lake, and this time the soldier seated himself by the eldest.

237

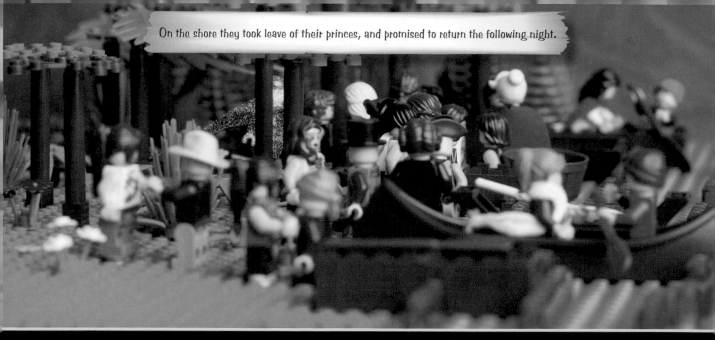

On the shore they took leave of their princes, and promised to return the following night.

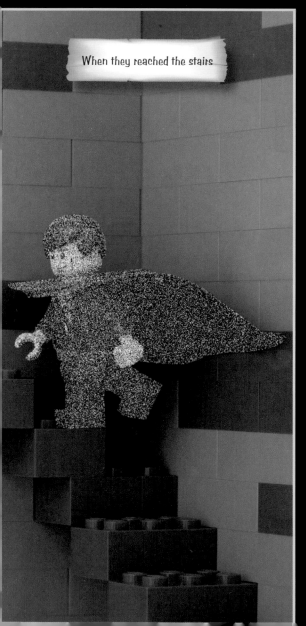

When they reached the stairs

the soldier ran on in front and lay down in his bed,

and when the twelve had come up slowly and wearily, he was already snoring so loudly that they could all hear him, and they said, "So far as he is concerned, we are safe."

They took off their beautiful dresses, laid them away,

put the worn-out shoes under the bed,

and lay down.

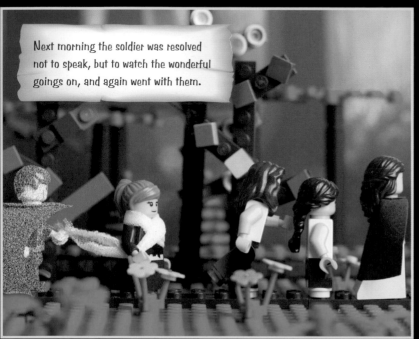
Next morning the soldier was resolved not to speak, but to watch the wonderful goings on, and again went with them.

Then everything was done just as it had been done the first time, and each time they danced until their shoes were worn to pieces.

But the third time he took a cup away with him as a token.

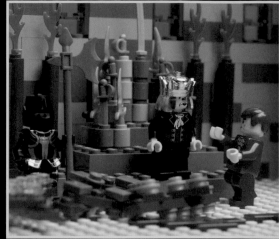

When the King put the question, "Where have my twelve daughters danced their shoes to pieces in the night?"

he answered, "In an underground castle with twelve princes,"

and related how it had come to pass,

and brought out the tokens.

The King then summoned his daughters,

and asked them if the soldier had told the truth,

and when they saw that they were betrayed, and that falsehood would be of no avail, they were obliged to confess all.

Thereupon the King asked which of them he would have to wife?

243

He answered, "I am no longer young, so give me the eldest."

Then the wedding was celebrated on the self-same day, and the kingdom was promised him after the King's death.

But the princes were bewitched for as many days as they had danced nights with the twelve.

King Thrushbeard

A King had a daughter who was beautiful beyond all measure, but so proud and haughty withal that no suitor was good enough for her. She sent away one after the other, and ridiculed them as well.

Once the King made a great feast and invited thereto, from far and near, all the young men likely to marry.

They were all marshalled in a row according to their rank and standing; first came the kings, then the grand-dukes, then the princes, the earls, the barons, and the gentry.

Then the King's daughter was led through the ranks, but to every one she had some objection to make; one was too fat, "The wine-cask," she said. Another was too tall, "Long and thin has little in." The third was too short, "Short and thick is never quick." The fourth was too pale, "As pale as death." The fifth too red, "A fighting-cock." The sixth was not straight enough, "A green log dried behind the stove."

So she had something to say against every one, but she made herself especially merry over a good king who stood quite high up in the row, and whose chin had grown a little crooked. "Well," she cried and laughed, "he has a chin like a thrush's beak!" and from that time he got the name of King Thrushbeard.

But the old King, when he saw that his daughter did nothing but mock the people, and despised all the suitors who were gathered there, was very angry, and swore that she should have for her husband the very first beggar that came to his doors.

247

A few days afterwards a fiddler came and sang beneath the windows, trying to earn a small alms. When the King heard him he said, "Let him come up."

So the fiddler came in, in his dirty, ragged clothes, and sang before the King and his daughter,

and when he had ended he asked for a trifling gift.

The King said, "Your song has pleased me so well that I will give you my daughter there, to wife."

The King's daughter shuddered, but the King said, "I have taken an oath to give you to the very first beggar-man, and I will keep it."

All she could say was in vain;

the priest was brought, and she had to let herself be wedded to the fiddler on the spot.

When that was done the King said, "Now it is not proper for you, a beggar-woman, to stay any longer in my palace, you may just go away with your husband."

The beggar-man led her out by the hand,

and she was obliged to walk away on foot with him.

When they came to a large forest she asked, "To whom does that beautiful forest belong?"

"It belongs to King Thrushbeard; if you had taken him, it would have been yours."

"Ah, unhappy girl that I am, if I had but taken King Thrushbeard!"

Afterwards they came to a meadow, and she asked again, "To whom does this beautiful green meadow belong?"

"It belongs to King Thrushbeard; if you had taken him, it would have been yours." "Ah, unhappy girl that I am, if I had but taken King Thrushbeard!"

Then they came to a large town, and she asked again, "To whom does this fine large town belong?"

"It belongs to King Thrushbeard; if you had taken him, it would have been yours." "Ah, unhappy girl that I am, if I had but taken King Thrushbeard!"

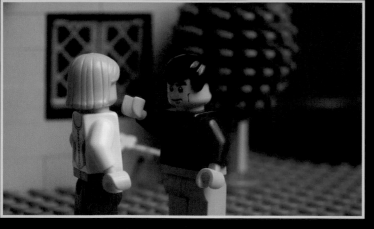

"It does not please me," said the fiddler, "to hear you always wishing for another husband; am I not good enough for you?"

At last they came to a very little hut, and she said, "Oh goodness! what a small house; to whom does this miserable, mean hovel belong?"

The fiddler answered, "That is my house and yours, where we shall live together."

She had to stoop in order to go in at the low door.

"Where are the servants?" said the King's daughter.

"What servants?" answered the beggar-man; "you must yourself do what you wish to have done. Just make a fire at once, and set on water to cook my supper, I am quite tired."

But the King's daughter knew nothing about lighting fires or cooking,

and the beggar-man had to lend a hand himself to get anything fairly done.

When they had finished their scanty meal they went to bed; but he forced her to get up quite early in the morning in order to look after the house.

253

For a few days they lived in this way as well as might be, and came to the end of all their provisions. Then the man said, "Wife, we cannot go on any longer eating and drinking here and earning nothing. You weave baskets." He went out, cut some willows, and brought them home.

Then she began to weave, but the tough willows wounded her delicate hands.

"I see that this will not do," said the man; "you had better spin, perhaps you can do that better."

She sat down and tried to spin, but the hard thread soon cut her soft fingers so that the blood ran down.

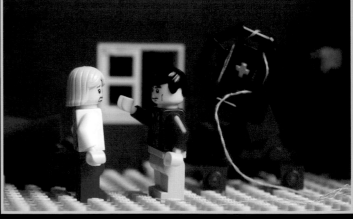

"See," said the man, "you are fit for no sort of work; I have made a bad bargain with you. Now I will try to make a business with pots and earthenware; you must sit in the market-place and sell the ware."

"Alas," thought she, "if any of the people from my father's kingdom come to the market and see me sitting there, selling, how they will mock me?"

But it was of no use, she had to yield unless she chose to die of hunger.

For the first time she succeeded well, for the people were glad to buy the woman's wares because she was good-looking, and they paid her what she asked;

many even gave her the money and left the pots with her as well. So they lived on what she had earned as long as it lasted, then the husband bought a lot of new crockery. With this she sat down at the corner of the market-place, and set it out round about her ready for sale.

But suddenly there came a drunken hussar galloping along, and he rode right amongst the pots so that they were all broken into a thousand bits.

She began to weep, and did now know what to do for fear. "Alas! what will happen to me?" cried she; "what will my husband say to this?"

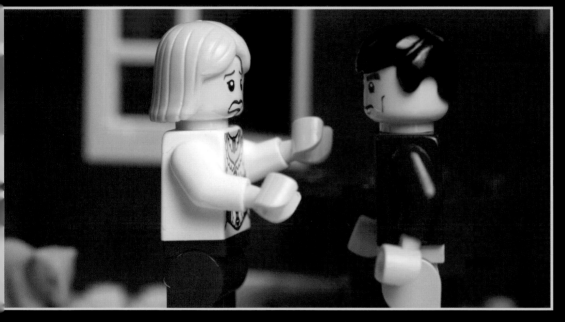

She ran home and told him of the misfortune. "Who would seat herself at a corner of the market-place with crockery?" said the man;

"leave off crying, I see very well that you cannot do any ordinary work, so I have been to our King's palace and have asked whether they cannot find a place for a kitchen-maid,

and they have promised me to take you; in that way you will get your food for nothing."

The King's daughter was now a kitchen-maid, and had to be at the cook's beck and call, and do the dirtiest work.

In both her pockets she fastened a little jar, in which she took home her share of the leavings, and upon this they lived.

It happened that the wedding of the King's eldest son was to be celebrated, so the poor woman went up and placed herself by the door of the hall to look on.

When all the candles were lit, and people, each more beautiful than the other, entered, and all was full of pomp and splendour, she thought of her lot with a sad heart,

and cursed the pride and haughtiness which had humbled her and brought her to so great poverty.

The smell of the delicious dishes which were being taken in and out reached her, and now and then the servants threw her a few morsels of them: these she put in her jars to take home.

All at once the King's son entered, clothed in velvet and silk, with gold chains about his neck.

And when he saw the beautiful woman standing by the door he seized her by the hand, and would have danced with her;

but she refused and shrank with fear,

for she saw that it was King Thrushbeard, her suitor whom she had driven away with scorn.

259

Her struggles were of no avail, he drew her into the hall; but the string by which her pockets were hung broke, the pots fell down, the soup ran out, and the scraps were scattered all about.

And when the people saw it, there arose general laughter and derision, and she was so ashamed that she would rather have been a thousand fathoms below the ground.

She sprang to the door and would have run away,

but on the stairs a man caught her and brought her back; and when she looked at him it was King Thrushbeard again. He said to her kindly, "Do not be afraid, I and the fiddler who has been living with you in that wretched hovel are one.

For love of you I disguised myself so; and I also was the hussar who rode through your crockery. This was all done to humble your proud spirit, and to punish you for the insolence with which you mocked me."

Then she wept bitterly and said, "I have done great wrong, and am not worthy to be your wife."

But he said, "Be comforted, the evil days are past; now we will celebrate our wedding."
Then the maids-in-waiting came and put on her the most splendid clothing,

and her father and his whole court came and wished her happiness in her marriage with King Thrushbeard, and the joy now began in earnest. I wish you and I had been there too.

ABOUT THE AUTHORS

Members of the Hollan Publishing team, John McCann, Monica Sweeney, and Becky Thomas all collaborated to make *Brick Fairy Tales* possible.

John McCann designed, constructed, and photographed the brick scenes. A New England native, John has over two decades of experience playing with LEGO bricks. He enjoys relaxing lakeside and can solve a Rubik's Cube in three days flat. John has a BS in biomedical engineering from the University of Hartford and is currently pursuing his masters. He is also the coauthor of *Brick Shakespeare: The Tragedies—Hamlet, Macbeth, Romeo and Juliet, and Julius Caesar, Brick Shakespeare: The Comedies—A Midsummer Night's Dream, The Tempest, Much Ado About Nothing, and The Taming of the Shrew, Loom Magic! 25 Awesome, Never-Before-Seen Designs for an Amazing Rainbow of Projects*, and *Loom Magic Xtreme!: 25 Spectacular, Never-Before-Seen Designs for Rainbows of Fun.*

Monica Sweeney helped select the Grimm fairy tales for construction and helped write the introduction. Monica loves all things related to Spain and Chaucer and has yet to say no to a mini powdered donut. She graduated with honors in English from the University of Massachusetts–Amherst. She is also the coauthor of *Brick Shakespeare: The Tragedies—Hamlet, Macbeth, Romeo and Juliet, and Julius Caesar, Brick Shakespeare: The Comedies—A Midsummer Night's Dream, The Tempest, Much Ado About Nothing, and The Taming of the Shrew*, and *Loom Magic Xtreme!: 25 Spectacular, Never-Before-Seen Designs for Rainbows of Fun.*

Becky Thomas helped select the Grimm fairy tales for construction and helped write the introduction. In her spare time, Becky enjoys breaking the bindings of all books Jane Austen, playing video games, and trying out new recipes. She graduated with honors in English from the University of Massuchesetts–Amherst, and she is also the coauthor of *Brick Shakespeare: The Tragedies—Hamlet, Macbeth, Romeo and Juliet, and Julius Caesar, Brick Shakespeare: The Comedies—A Midsummer Night's Dream, The Tempest, Much Ado About Nothing, and The Taming of the Shrew, Loom Magic! 25 Awesome, Never-Before-Seen Designs for an Amazing Rainbow of Projects*, and *Loom Magic Xtreme!: 25 Spectacular, Never-Before-Seen Designs for Rainbows of Fun.*

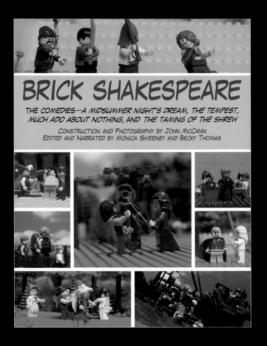

Brick Shakespeare

The Comedies—*A Midsummer Night's Dream, The Tempest, Much Ado About Nothing,* and *The Taming of the Shrew*

Construction and Photography by John McCann
Edited and Narrated by Monica Sweeney and Becky Thomas

Explore four of Shakespeare's comedies like never before—with LEGO bricks! This book presents Shakespeare's most delightful comedies, *A Midsummer Night's Dream, Much Ado About Nothing, The Taming of the Shrew,* and *The Tempest,* in one thousand amazing color photographs. This unique adaptation of the world's most famous plays stays true to Shakespeare's original text, while giving audiences an exciting new perspective as the stories are retold with the universally beloved construction toy.

Get caught up in hilarious misadventures as brick Puck leads the lovers astray through the brick forests of Athens. Watch Cupid kill with traps in the plot to marry Beatrice and Benedick. Marvel at the changing disguises of the men vying for brick Bianca's affections, and feel the churn of the ocean as Prospero sinks his brother's ship into the brick sea. These iconic stories jump off the page with fun, creative sets built brick by brick, scene by scene!

This incredible method of storytelling gives new life to Shakespeare's masterpieces. With an abridged form that maintains original Shakespearean language and modern visuals, this ode to the Bard is sure to please all audiences, from the most versed Shakespeare enthusiasts to young students and newcomers alike!

$19.95 Paperback • ISBN 978-1-62873-733-2

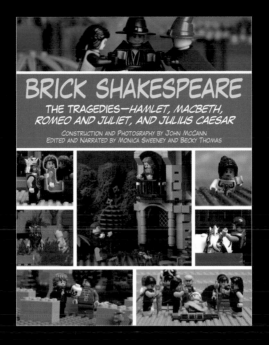

Brick Shakespeare

The Tragedies—Hamlet, Macbeth, Romeo and Juliet, and Julius Caesar

Construction and Photography by John McCann
Edited and Narrated by Monica Sweeney and Becky Thomas

Enjoy four of Shakespeare's tragedies told with LEGO bricks. Here are *Hamlet*, *Macbeth*, *Romeo and Juliet*, and *Julius Caesar* enacted scene by scene, captioned by excerpts from the plays. Flip through one thousand color photographs as you enjoy Shakespeare's iconic poetry and marvel at what can be done with the world's most popular children's toy.

Watch brick Hamlet give his famous "To be or not to be" soliloquy, and feel brick Ophelia's grief as she meets her watery end. Lady Macbeth in brick form brings new terror to "Out, out, damn spot!" and brick Romeo and Juliet are no less star-crossed for being rectangular and plastic. The warm familiarity of bricks lends levity to Shakespeare's tragedies while remaining true to his original language.

The ideal book for Shakespeare enthusiasts, as well as a fun way to introduce children to Shakespeare's masterpieces, this book employs Shakespeare's original, characteristic language in abridged form. Though the language stays true to its origins, the unique format of these well-known tragedies will give readers a new way to enjoy one of the most popular playwrights in history.

$19.95 Paperback • ISBN 978-1-62636-303-8

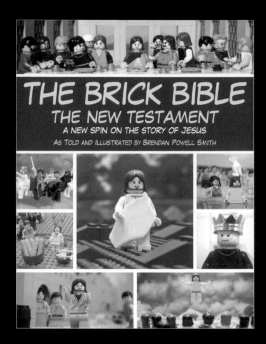

The Brick Bible: The New Testament
A New Spin on the Story of Jesus
by Brendan Powell Smith

From the author of the highly praised and somewhat controversial *The Brick Bible: A New Spin on the Old Testament* comes the much-anticipated New Testament edition. For over a decade, Brendan Powell Smith, creator of popular website bricktestament.com, has been hard at work using LEGO to re-create scenes from the Bible. Now, in one volume, he has brought together over 1,000 "brick" photographs depicting the narrative story of the New Testament. From the life of Jesus—his birth, teachings, and parables—to the famous last supper scene and the crucifixion; from the fate of Judas to the life of Paul and his letters to the Ephesians; from the first book burning to the book of Revelations, this is the New Testament as you've never experienced it before.

Smith combines the actual text of the New Testament with his brick photographs to bring to life the teachings, miracles, and prophecies of the most popular book in the world. The graphic novel format makes these well-known Bible stories come to life in a fun and engaging way. And the beauty of *The Brick Bible: The New Testament* is that everyone, from the devout to nonbelievers, will find something breathtaking, fascinating, or entertaining within this impressive collection.

$19.95 Paperback • ISBN 978-1-62087-1-720

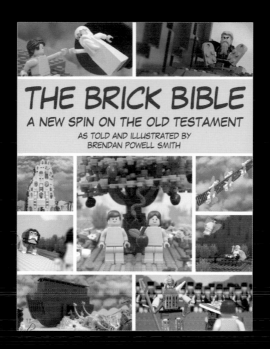

The Brick Bible

A New Spin on the Old Testament

by Brendan Powell Smith

Brendan Powell Smith has spent the last decade creating nearly 5,000 scenes from the bible—with Legos. His wonderfully original sets are featured on his website, Bricktestament.com, but for the first time, 1,500 photographs of these creative designs—depicting the Old Testament from Earth's creation to the Books of Kings—are brought together in book format. The Holy Bible is complex; sometimes dark, and other times joyous, and Smith's masterful work is a far cry from what a small child might build. The beauty of The Brick Bible is that everyone, from the devout to nonbelievers, will find something breathtaking, fascinating, or entertaining within this collection. Smith's subtle touch brings out the nuances of each scene and makes you reconsider the way you look at LEGOs—it's something that needs to be seen to be believed.

$19.95 Paperback · ISBN 978-1-61608-421-9

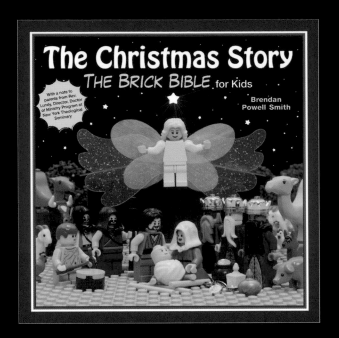

The Christmas Story
The Brick Bible for Kids
by Brendan Powell Smith

Santa, sleigh bells, mistletoe, reindeer, and presents: these are the tell-tale signs of Christmas. But for Christians, December 25 is also the time to celebrate the birth of Jesus, and what better way to introduce your kids to the story of the Savior's birth than through LEGO!

Every year, children of all ages revisit the scene in Bethlehem with Joseph, Mary, the three wise men, the angels and shepherds, and the baby Jesus, swaddled and lying in a manger. Kids will love seeing the story of Christmas played out using their favorite toys. Brendan Powell Smith, author of The Brick Bible for Kids series—beginning with *Noah's Ark*—creates a magical "brick" world around the simplified text of the Immaculate Conception, the census, the guiding star high above Bethlehem, and the promise one little baby brings to the Christians of the world. This important Christmas story is sure to be the perfect holiday gift and a book for families to cherish for years to come.

$12.95 Hardcover • ISBN 978-1-62087-173-7

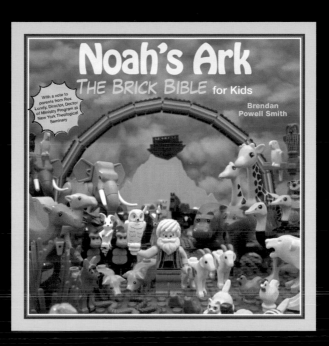

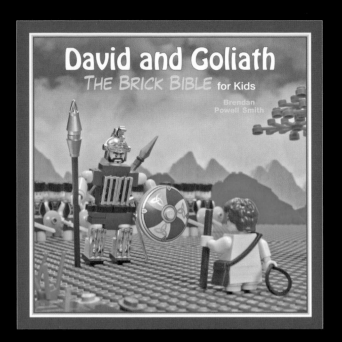

David and Goliath
The Brick Bible for Kids
by Brendan Powell Smith

The Philistine army has gathered for a vicious war against King Saul and the Israelites. With great suspense, a Philistine giant named Goliath boldly approaches the Israelites presenting a challenge: Defeat him and the Philistines will forever be their slaves; but if the Israelites lose, then they must become slaves to the Philistines. But who would want to defy such a giant, wearing only the finest armor and carrying the sharpest spear?

Nearby, a young boy named David is told to bring food to his older brothers in the army. When he arrives, he hears of Goliath's challenge. He offers to face the giant by himself. Goliath is convinced this must be some joke. But don't underestimate young David! Enjoy reading one of the Bible's best stories illustrated in LEGO as a family.

$12.95 Hardcover • ISBN 978-1-62087-982-5

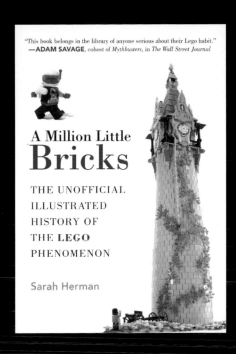

A Million Little Bricks

The Unofficial Illustrated History of the LEGO Phenomenon

by Sarah Herman

There aren't many titles that haven't been bestowed on LEGO toys, and it's not hard to see why. From its inception in the early 1930s right up until today, the LEGO Group's history is as colorful as the toys it makes. Few other playthings share the LEGO brand's creative spirit, educative benefits, resilience, quality, and universal appeal. The LEGO name is now synonymous with playtime, but it wasn't always so. This history charts the birth of the LEGO Group in the workshop of a Danish carpenter and its steady growth as a small, family-run toy manufacturer to its current position as a market-leading, award-winning brand. The company's ever-increasing catalog of products—including the earliest wooden toys, plastic bricks, play themes, and other building systems such as DUPLO, Technic, and MINDSTORMS—are chronicled in detail, alongside the manufacturing process, LEGOLAND parks, licensed toys, and computer and video games.

Learn all about how LEGO pulled itself out of an economic crisis and embraced technology to make building blocks relevant to twenty-first-century children, and discover the vibrant fan community of kids and adults whose conventions, websites, and artwork keep the LEGO spirit alive. As nostalgic as it is contemporary, *A Million Little Bricks* will have you reminiscing about old Classic Space sets, rummaging through the attic for forgotten Minifigure friends, and playing with whatever LEGO bricks you can get your hands on (even if it means sharing with your kids).

$16.95 Paperback • ISBN 978-1-62636-118-8

ALSO AVAILABLE

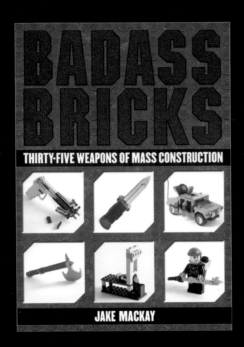

Badass Bricks
Thirty-Five Weapons of Mass Construction
by Jack Mackay

LEGO is fun. So are toy weapons. The only thing more fun is LEGO toy weapons! A compilation of badass brick weapons—some that actually even work—this book is designed for the adult brick enthusiast. Each project is original (i.e., not from a LEGO kit) and is accompanied by how-to schematics and full-color original photographs of the finished object. Dangerous and exciting projects include:

- Tomahawk
- Broadsword
- Claymore (two-handed sword)
- Ninja throwing star
- M1911 pistol
- Siege tower
- Gatling gun
- MK2 grenade
- Scythed chariot
- Paris gun
- Flamethrower
- And many more!

Hobbyists love to make weapons, and this book goes far beyond the kits that are available to showcase forty projects for amazing weapons. The projects range from medieval to modern, from small hand grenades to an actual working guillotine to an assault amphibious vehicle. *Badass Bricks* will keep adults occupied for hours and is the perfect book for the adult brick enthusiast, weapons hobbyist, or all-around badass!

$17.95 Paperback · ISBN 978-1-62636-304-5